The Ibiza Diaries

Also by Grace Dent

DIARY OF A CHAV
Trainers V. Tiaras
Slinging the Bling
Too Cool for School

The Ibiza Diaries

Grace Dent

A division of Hachette Children's Books

Copyright © 2008 Grace Dent

First published in Great Britain in 2008
by Hodder Children's Books

4

A Catalogue record for this book is available from the British Library

ISBN-13: 978 0 340 97063 8

Typeset in New Baskerville by Avon DataSet Ltd,
Bidford-on-Avon, Warwickshire

Printed in the UK by CPI Bookmarque, Croydon, CR0 4TD

The paper and board used in this paperback by Hodder Children's Books
are natural recyclable products made from wood grown in
sustainable forests. The manufacturing processes conform to the
environmental regulations of the country of origin.

Hodder Children's Books
A division of Hachette Children's Books
338 Euston Road, London NW1 3BH
An Hachette Livre UK Company

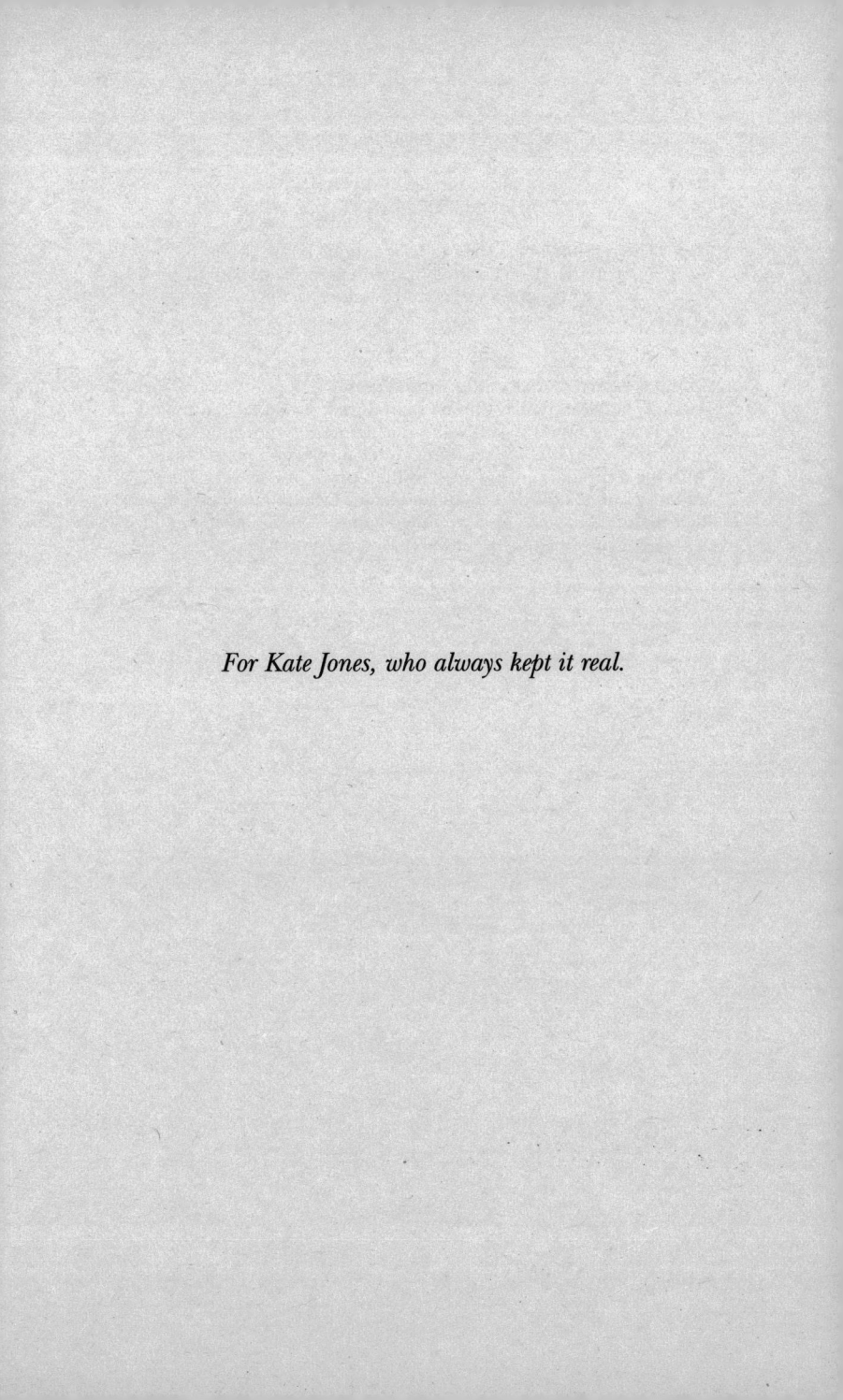

For Kate Jones, who always kept it real.

This diary belongs to:

Lady Shiznizz Woodizzle

Address: 34, Thundizzle Road,
Goodmayes,
Essex,
BRAP 100

JUNE

FRIDAY 4TH JUNE

10pm – Fin's Room. (Formerly known as Shiraz Bailey Wood's room) Thundershizzle Road, Goodmayes, Essex.

TEN PROPER MINTAGE THINGS ABOUT SHIZZLEBIZZLE WOOD FLYING OFF TO IBIZA FOR HER TWO WEEK SUNSHINE HOLIDAY!!!!!

1. Me, Carrie Draper, Uma Brunton-Fletcher and Kezia Marshall are all going together!! Yes, to Ibiza! The Ibiza you always hear about on the TV and everywhere and we're sharing an apartment!! Brap brap brapppppage! AND our friends Sean and Danny are flying out later to meet us!

2. Ibiza will be a proper amazing holiday with clubbing and sunbathing and bare choong boys and cocktails and all-night non-stop mentaloidism – just like on Sky One's *Ibiza X-Rated* and Bravo TV's *Ibiza: Boobs Uncovered!* Except we'll be a lot better behaved than that obviously 'cos we are all good girls. HONEST MOTHER IF YOU ARE READING THIS ON YOUR LUNCH HOUR EATING YOUR BLOODY SPAGHETTI HOOPS ON TOAST, AS USUAL.

3. The weather will be red hot in Ibiza. Like what summer is MEANT to be and NOT like it actually is in Goodmayes, Essex, where it has pissed it down for the last month. Well, except for last Thursday when the sun popped out for twenty minutes and Bert at Number 89 sat out on his doorstep in his ancient underpants which looked like they were from the Victorian era 'cos they were like well yellow and it was so minging I still get sick explosions in my throat just thinking 'bout it.

4. In our apartment I will have a REAL BED to sleep in. NOT a bloody blow-up bed with a puncture in it like I'm sleeping on now at 34 Thundersley Road!

Oh my dayz!!! I still can't bloody believe Cava-Sue gave my bed away when I was in London! She says it was to make more room for 'Fin's stuff'. What stuff? He's only bloody seven months old! What does he need space for? His darts trophies? His flatscreen Blu-Ray plasma TV? I wouldn't mind so bloody much if she'd got some proper cash for it, but OH NO – she put it in the FREECYCLE section of the *Ilford Bugle* and gave it away!! Which bloody reminds me . . .

5. In Ibiza I won't be able to hear Cava-Sue quacking on about saving the planet. HURRAH. I can't believe I actually missed her when I was in London 'cos she's been a major arse-ache since she began her job as an 'environmental officer' for Goodmayes Council, working

sixteen hours a week at nine pounds per hour to nag folk about what they do with their tin cans. She's got a badge and uniform and everything!

I can just about cope with Cava-Sue sticking her face against the loo door, reminding me I only need two sheets to wipe when I am having a wazz, but YESTERDAY she found a load of cardboard Tampax inner tubes in my bin and she says, ''Ere, Shiz!! What a waste of natural resources this is!! Can't you make a necklace out of them or something?'

So I goes, 'Nice one, Cava-Sue, that's well a good idea, innit! And after that I might get some of Mother's old used Always Ultras and make the dry weave top sheets into an head band! 'Ere, I bet them people who run Claire's Accessories will be crapping themselves when they hear about it. Their business will be in shreds!'

So then Cava-Sue goes, 'Oh, whatever, Shiraz, why don't you shut your trap and just do one with your negative vibes!?' So I says, ''Ere Cava-Sue, no, why don't YOU shut your trap? And ANYWAYS I'm off to Ibiza next week, sis, so you won't hear me being negative then WILL YOU?!' So Cava-Sue says, 'Oh shut up jabbering on about Ibiza! Shut up!' Then Mum walked in and told us both to bloody shut our traps 'cos we were more of a pain in the rear end now than when we were babies.

It's not me who starts it. It's bloody CAVA-SUE!!
(Awww – I love her really – she's my big sister, innit?)

6. WESLEY BARRINGTON BAINS II. In Ibiza I will not have to think about my ex-boyfriend Wesley. Well, sort of 'ex', 'cos I still love him a bit but I'm not IN LOVE with him 'cos he ain't that buff or nothing and he can't handle me being so real and wanting to experience life and all that. Yagetme?

So anyway, I've told my Wesley this about 137 times and now he's got the hump and started going out with this girl called Sooz who works as a shop assistant in Boots the Chemist in Ilford and who is so bloody kill-yourself BORING that when you go to Boots you can't even tell whether you've met the real Sooz or one of those cardboard cut-out shop assistants they put on the end of aisles to try and stop kids thieving the condoms. And she wears cropped jackets from Per Una at Marks and Spencer like she's thirty-bloody-five or something and her hair is frazzly and dry like old woman's pubes that have been GHD straightened.

Not that I care anyway, Wesley. I don't care at all. I hope you're happy with Sooz and her pube-head. And don't think I miss you or nothing or that I go on your Bebo and look at your photos or comments or try and work out what you're up to 'cos I don't. EVAH. As from today. That's it. THE END.

7. Anyway, in Ibiza there will be LOADS OF OTHER BOYS AND ME AND MY CREW CAN HAVE A LAUGH WITH THEM AND SNOG THEM AND GO MENTAL!!!

I am well excited about this! OK, not as excited as Carrie, who to be honest, can be a bit of a hooch when she wants to be and NO WAY AT ALL as totally mentally frothing at the mouth with excitement as Kezia who keeps sending me proper FILTHY texts going on about how much she's looking forward to 'getting it every night'. Now this is a worry as she's already got one bloody baby and I was hoping she might have a bit more sense by now and ain't going to end up coming home from Ibiza 'with a belly full of arms and legs' as my mother tutted this morning.

Mother doesn't want me to go to Ibiza with Kezia. She is trying every way going to stop it. Yesterday she tried to get me to cancel it by saying she'd just been up Chadwell Heath to see Nan and she reckons Nan was looking 'not long for this world with blue lips and it might be an idea if I took Nan and Clement for a week in a caravan in Reigate instead'!!!

Ha ha ha! Reigate! LMAO!

There is absolutely nothing wrong with Nan. Nan is proper supportive of me going to Ibiza! In fact she gave me twenty quid to buy some of 'those cocktails they set fire to what makes you dance with your top off'. Nan says she wishes she was 'young and daft again with knees that didn't swell up and friends who would rather dance than bleeding well drop dead all the time, the bloody miserable sods!'

So there you have it. IBIZA IS GOING TO BE

AH-MAY-ZING!!! I cannot bloody wait. ONLY THREE MORE SLEEPS TILL WE GO!!!

1am – Oh God.

I can't bloody sleep. I feel a bit sick. I wish I'd never started thinking about all this Ibiza stuff.

I'm worrying a bit now. It's times like this when I miss living with Uma 'cos she's proper practical about stuff and sort of chills me down. She's a good listener too.

That was the most rubbish thing about leaving London and moving back to Goodmayes: leaving Uma in the flat to get new flatmates. She lives with two Polish girls now. It's well good that she's taking two weeks off work at the casino to come to Ibiza! And when she flies home she's starting a new job at one of Mr Deng's other casinos, The Fortune Club, over in West London. This job's got live-in accomodation too! Uma is doing brilliant for herself, innit. I keep telling other Goodmayes folk how Uma has proper sorted herself out now, but no one believes me. That's 'cos if you don't know her well Uma can give out this nasty-girl vibe, like she's planning to have you skinned and made into a lampshade. But the truth is Uma's a grafter when she puts her mind to it. Total respect to Uma.

Anyway, I'm gonna make a list of my worries to tell her.

IBIZA THINGS WHAT I AM WORRIED ABOUT:

1. Ibiza is a proper LONG WAY AWAY.
We have to get a train, then a plane then a bus to the hotel! It takes like SIX whole hours to get there and it looks proper complicated and I'm not being funny or nothing but last time me and Uma and Carrie and Kezia went anywhere further than Ilford Xchange together, well it ended in COMPLETE DISASTER. 'Cos that was Year 9 when we went to Alton Towers and it was bare jokes for a bit and then Uma got done by security for sparking up a proper smelly joint of White Widow skunk in the Log Flume queue and spent the rest of the day in Alton Towers' prison listening to Mayflower Academy teachers and security guards arguing about what class drug cannabis was and whether they needed to get the real police. And then Miss Bunt the English teacher caught Kezia letting this lad she met called Ataf from Margate feel her boobs up in the Haunted House and Miss Bunt went TOTALLY SCHIZOID MENTAL and that was sort of the start of Miss Bunt having the nervo breakdown and wanting to go back to Adelaide in Australia and be a florist.

Saying that, maybe this was good for Miss Bunt 'cos the other day me and Carrie found her MySpace page and she'd put up a photo of her in Australia holding a big bunch of flowers and smiling and she'd even got rid of her moustache, so maybe us acting like nutjobs all the way through Year 9 was a good thing.

Anyway that was a long time ago. When we were all immature. Now that we are all eighteen we're gonna be well grown up on our trip to Ibiza.

2. In Ibiza I ain't got no choice but to wear a BIKINI. And this is well doing my head in 'cos my body just ain't a bikini kind of body. I don't look nothing like that Paris Hilton or Lindsey Lohan do when you see pics of them in *Heat* on holiday.

I ain't smooth and shiny. I've got puffy skin and quite thick arms and legs and my body is sort of spud-shaped, a bit like Upsy-Daisy from *In The Night Garden*. And as for going topless and letting my baps all hang out, well that DEFINITELY AIN'T happening, right? 'Cos despite the fact that I have prayed to Baby Jesus in heaven about two hundred times on the tits subject since I was fourteen I still have flat nipples that ONLY poke out when it is sub-zero conditions. Not proper sticky out ones like Carrie Draper has. Proper nobbly ones that can make Domino Pizza delivery blokes accidently ride their moped into a hedge when she wears a white crop top. Yagetme?

But worse than that, over the last year I seem to have started to get PROPER HAIRY. My pubes have had a mentalist fit and started growing in a line up to my belly button! And I'm finding long hairs behind my knees! And curly ones on the sides of my thighs! OMG it is the most minging thing ever. Anyway, I tells our Cava-Sue about this and she cracks up for half an hour and starts calling me 'baboon flaps' and then she gets sensible and says, 'Oh for God's sake, Shizza, it's called being a WOMAN! Women have hair, we're not meant to be bald like little girls! That is just another stupid paranoia invented by women's magazines.'

Well this didn't make me feel any better so then Cava-Sue said, ''Ere, Shiz, you should remember that there are areas of Khazakistan in Central Asia where hairy women are considered very attractive.'

'That's made me feel a lot better, Cava-Sue, thanks,' I said.

I'm buying some Veet wax strips tomorrow. We're going to Ibiza not Khazakihairybushistan, we don't have to flounce about with knicker-forests like Sulley from Monsters Inc.

3. THE MURPHY PROBLEM.

I'm worried about my little brother Murphy. He is well broken-hearted about his girlfriend Ritu going back to Japan. Thing is, Murphy ain't been talking much lately. And it's not like he keeps a diary or anything like I do, to get any of this stuff out of his system. I dunno what I'd do without my diary, I'm always nipping off and scribbling in it. It proper sorts my head out.

Murphy just sits in his room and listens to dubstep most nights. And not happy dubstep or nothing. Really heavy trippy dubstep that sounds like someone inside a wheelie bin eating crisps mixed with samples of babies crying and church bells and opera singing and weird shit like that over a 142 bpm nosebleed drumbeat. And when he's not listening to dubstep he's sitting about with a face like old chipfat or he's hanging about with Tariq and Sizzle from his class in Year 11 and chatting all this gangster shit about how 'him and his bredren can't even go to Londis for a can of coke 'cos Londis ain't in their postcode so they might get merked by a rival gang'.

OH MY LIFE, what a load of old crap. I just walked to Londis tonight to get a scratchcard. I didn't see no rival gangs 'trespassing in our endz' at all. The only person I saw was Mrs Reema who moaned for twenty minutes about the shocking state of Old Bert's underpants.

So anyway, last night I asks Murphy what he's up to and he says he was waiting for Sizzle to come over 'cos 'Thundersley Road Man Dem' were meeting up to chat about 'ting. THE THUNDERSLEY ROAD MAN DEM?? I'm not happy 'bout Murphy and Tariq giving their gang a name 'cos this is how stupid gangster shit starts. It starts as a game like playing soldiers then ends with someone getting stabbed.

I felt better later when I found out the Man Dem weren't meeting after all 'cos Tariq had promised his mother he'd help do the big shop at Lidl and Sizzle was doing his Religious Studies coursework instead.

Brap, brap, brap.

4. SILLY FAT PENNY MY STAFFY

While we're in Ibiza my mother has agreed to look after Uma's Staffy, Zeus. And I know Zeus is going to be well spoiled and all that 'cos mum LOVES Staffies, but it's our Pen who is worrying me a bit 'cos of what happened the other day when Uma brought Zeus over for a 'trial visit'.

OH MY LIFE, Penny started making a right show of herself. She proper fell in love. It turns out that Zeus is like the Zac Efron of the Staffy world! He is a bare choong Staffy. Obviously, me and Uma can't see this, what with us not being bull terriers ourselves. So the moment Zeus arrives, our Penny went a bit mental and spent the whole time lying on her back with her paws in the air being a proper hoochiemomma! And I mean a hundred per cent Latoya Bell 'no knickers showing her pink bits' hoochiemomma. It was well shameful.

Worse thing of all, Zeus proper blanked Pen. He just ate the Chicken Tikka Pukka pie we'd bought him, pretending Penny was invisible! I reckon Pen just ain't his type. Maybe this is 'cos she is like proper certifiable clinically obese and makes snorty sounds when she walks and completely refuses to go outside for a widdle until I leave a trail of Nice 'n' Spicy Nik Naks out as far as the wheeliebin then run in quick and slam the door. Poor Pen. She's gonna get her heart broken.

NOTE: must speak to Carrie and see where we can buy Penny a pair of doggie knickers to cover her 'pink bits'.

Carrie will know this 'cos her chihuahua Alexis has got loads of stupid outifts. It's the only dog I've ever seen squeezing a poo out with a fake Louis Vuitton handbag stuck to its paw.

5. WHAT HAPPENS AFTER IBIZA?

My proper biggest worry about Ibiza is that it's only two weeks out of my whole life. And so when I get back I've got to be the bloody master of my destiny all over again. I can't believe that I still don't know what I'm gonna do with my life.

Mother keeps saying I should get down to that greasy café Mr Yolk and tell Mario I'll be back from Ibiza soon and I want my old job back again washing plates and frying eggs.

I pretend to be deaf when Mum says that. I can't bloody tell her that I went down Mr Yolk's last Tuesday and found this really chatty, pretty blonde-haired Polish girl called Agnieszka serving behind the counter where I used to stand. And this Agnieszka bird was being proper smiley and quick at serving! And never, not once, did she mouth, 'Oh piss off, Mario, you munter,' when he was nagging her to fry eggs quicker. And this Agnieszka was giving people the right change first time and everything and counting it up in her head without even using the till! And at no point did bloody goody-two-shoes Agnieszka get caught with the nozzle of the Anchor squirty dairy cream in her gob, filling it up while texting

16

Carrie Draper and windin' her waist to classic dancehall on Rude FM.

And when I asked Mario if there was any chance of getting my old job back he just laughed and said, 'Oh, Shirelle, you funny girl!' and he laughs so hard I thought I was going to see widdle leaking through his chef's pants. What a bloody cheek?! My Wesley Barrington Bains II is right about that whole Polish immigration thingy, innit? They're coming over here doing jobs us British folk used to take pride in!! It's TOTALLY unfair!!

But if I don't go back to Mr Yolk what am I going to do??! Go back and finish my A Levels? Go travelling? Go back to London? Try and make myself be properly in love with Wesley even though that would mean stealing him off bloody Sooz and ignoring that there is a patch of baldness poking through his hair what looks like a UFO landing pad?

Or what??

WHAT AM I GOING TO DO???

3am – OK, have just been on MSN chatting with Carrie. Carrie says that I've gotta stop being such a pain in the ringpiece about all this Ibiza business and just pack my bikini and some wax strips for my bush and get on the bloody aeroplane and shut up 'cos it is going to be MENTAL and BARE JOKES and MINTAGE and ROFL AND LOL X 1 MILLION etc., etc. Carrie says the whole point of Ibiza is to go there and free your mind and experience an Ibizan sunset and FIND YOURSELF. Carrie reckons that when we get to Ibiza and see the sunset everything will become clear and all our problems will be over for ever.

I love Carrie Draper. She is batshit crazy most of the time but at least you know where you stand with her.

IBIZA HERE WE COME!!!

SATURDAY 5TH JUNE

12pm – THREE MORE SLEEPS UNTIL IBIZA – WOOT WOOT WOOT!

If I ever get any proper sleep that is. That bloody blow-up mattress I'm sleeping on is well C to the R to the A to the P.

It only had about two breaths of air in it by 7am this morning. There's gotta be another puncture in it somewhere 'cos it was hissing all night long and I woke up face down in the carpet with a gobfull of fluff. Obviously at this point I remembered how PROPER HAPPY I was about Cava-Sue inviting some bloody hippy over to STEAL MY BLOODY BED.

I was gonna start kicking off at Cava-Sue about it this morning but I decided not to 'cos it was her day off work and she looked proper knackered. This whole having a job and having a baby at the same time thing is a proper headbend, I reckon. Cava-Sue says that when she goes to work she feels all guilty for leaving Fin. But then when she's at home she misses being at work 'cos at work she can talk to grown-ups and not just watch Macca Pacca and Igglepiggle floating about a bloody garden in a boat all day. Cava-Sue says she don't know why she bothers 'cos she feels like a bad mother whatever she does. Cava-Sue ain't a bad mother. Fin is a well smiley kid most of the time. As long as he's got clean pants and a jar of that minging Cow and Gate 'Vegetable Medley' stuff that looks like runny bellybutton wax, well it's happy days.

Cava-Sue is proper extra exhausted this week 'cos she's been sorting out this big argument about recycling boxes over on Bridge Avenue. It has turned into RECYCLING BOX WAR! Apparently Goodmayes council will only let every house have two boxes BUT everyone needs LOADS more than two boxes so they're all thieving them off each other in the middle of the night!! HA HA HA. LMAO! Well anyway, last Thursday the bloke at Number 12 got proper ANGRY about this and he stole FOUR boxes back in the middle of the night then spray-painted big pink willies on the side of them and his house number! BIG PINK WILLIES! With some sort of, erm, stuff dribbling out of the end. Ha ha ha! Well, no one wanted the pink willy boxes back then but Number 14 reported willie-man to the police and he ended up with a caution for 'offensive grafitti'. So then willie man's missus went MENTAL and chucked a box over her neighbour's garden fence almost squashing their terrier dog and then everyone started fighting and Cava-Sue had to split up two grown women in dressing gowns pulling each other's hair and calling each other 'thieving slags'. OH MY LIFE! Ha ha ha!

Cava-Sue looked sad when she told me this story. So I says, "'Ere, Cava-Sue, why don't you just give everyone more boxes if they need them?' Then Cava-Sue got the hump and says, 'Shiraz! If we give everyone more boxes they'll just fill them up and we are supposed to be CUTTING DOWN ON WASTE AREN'T WE?!!!' And then she stormed upstairs leaving Dad holding Fin, slamming her bedroom door and putting on some emo CD by her new favourite band 'There Is No Emoticon Available To Express My Misery'.

Well, me and Dad started howling. But we waited till the music started 'cos to be honest we're both a bit scared of Cava-Sue when she is knackered. This is ever since that time two weeks back when Lewis tried to suggest that Cava-Sue wasn't holding Fin properly so Cava-Sue threw a chair at Lewis and stormed out the front door and sat smoking rollies on Mrs Reema's wall wearing pyjama bottoms and a T-shirt covered in baby spew.

'Cos that's the thing about having babies. They just come into your world and spread joy, innit.

11pm – Just been to Draperville to chat to Carrie about Ibiza. I am well excited now!!

Draperville was bare jokes as ever. To be honest, it's always a laugh just watching Carrie being totally blonde and her dad Barney and her mum Diane floating round that funny big house what's well too massive for them with the white carpets and gold statues, trying to be all lah-di-dah posh when they're not really posh at all. They're just like the Wood family, quite common. 'They just got bloody lucky!' my mother was saying tonight AGAIN as I was putting my hoodie on to leave. 'And if you see that Maria Draper,' my mum was saying, 'ask her about that party we all had at Goodmayes Social in 1981 where she drank too much Babycham and had her knickers on her head GUSSET SIDE OUT dancing to Dire Straits! Ask her! Maria don't mention that when she's filling that trolley to the brim in Marks and Spencer foodhall wearing those white trousers thinking she's bloody Princess Diana, does she? Eh?!!!' 'True, Mother,' I said. 'She don't.'

There's something about Maria Draper that jars my mother's head good and proper. I think it's 'cos Maria is always well calm and tanned with nice toenails and clothes, while my mother wears big cardigans made of shiny wool out of George at ASDA and has proper long jaggy toenails and big toes that are a bit hairy. Whenever I give her a pedicure I tell her they look a bit like the Honey Monster's and Mum always laughs.

Thing is, I'd rather have my mum than Carrie's mum any day 'cos I love my mother proper loads. I mean, she drives me mental half the time, but she's still my mum and you only get one mum don't you? (Well unless you're

Shaznay Barret in my class at Mayflower, 'cos her real mum turned lezbitarian and ran off with her water aerobics instructor and then Shaznay had about three more mums after that 'cos her dad was a proper nightmare who couldn't keep his wotsit in his trousers. I know that 'cos my mother told me. See, that's why I love my mum, she knows everything.)

So, anyways I get round to Carrie's house and Barney is in the front drive by the big wrought-iron gates with 'DRAPERVILLE' written on them except it don't say Draperville no more 'cos Carrie's smashed into the gates in her Golf GTI while getting a driving lesson this morning. So Barney's looking a bit cheesed off, 'cos not only is he now paying for a new rear light for Carrie's car, he's now living in a house called 'RAPERVILLE', which don't exactly sound like a nice place to live at all. LMAO!!! Me and Carrie were wetting ourselves 'bout this all night imagining what Raperville would look like. Like a big spooky house full of blokes off *Crimewatch* with wild staring eyes all rattling the gates to get out going RRRRROOOAR!!! Ha ha ha! So then Carrie tells Maria our joke and Maria says that we shouldn't say that no more as the joke wasn't funny. I was gonna tell Maria to lighten up and have a Babycham and another go dancing with her knickers on her head but I didn't. Sometimes I put 'keeping it real' on hold these days just to keep the peace.

Carrie pretended she wanted me to come over tonight

'cos she wanted to wax my downstairs hairy bits for me, but that wasn't true at all. Really, she got me over to play bloody Singstar with her 'cos Barney has just bought her the new Pop Volume 9 disc from ASDA to help her get over 'the trauma of her car crash'. CAR CRASH!!! She'd only reversed five metres backwards into his bloody gates!!

Carrie LOVES Singstar though. She loves it. She reckons that she wants to be a singer one hundred and ten per cent now, not a beautician like she did last year. She'll stand there for three hours on the go singing her head off. Carrie's neighbours over the fence don't love Singstar that much though. They complained twice this month already and then got some lawyer geezer to write Barney Wood a letter requesting Carrie to 'cease and desist' from her 'anti-social behaviour'. Ha ha ha. Too much jokes. Barney Wood just laughed at the letter too. Barney says it's not his fault if those 'deaf prats can't appreciate solid gold talent right on their doorstep'. Barney says they'll feel stupid when they're round begging for tickets when Carrie plays the O2 Arena.

Well, when I got to Carrie's room this evening she was halfway through 'The Sweetest Thing' by Gwen Stefani, proper giving it both barrels doing the high notes and the woo-yeahs and everything. It didn't sound like solid gold talent to be frank. It reminded me of that time in Year 8 when Uma Brunton-Fletcher set fire to Sonia

Cathcarts's 'Jesus Christ is Everywhere' bumbag with Sonia still wearing it.

Carrie is proper hyped about Ibiza, she reckons there's loads of karaoke bars in San Antonio where we're staying. Carrie says Ibiza is where loads of DJs and bands and music bods go on holiday so it will be good place to 'meet the right people and get spotted'. I said ''Ere, Carrie, we certainly got "spotted" when we went on that ITV2 *Million Dollar Talent* show didn't we? That bloody judge said me and you were so funny looking we reminded him of "the Chuckle Brothers let loose in Primark"! It was well shameful.'

Well Carrie made a face when I said that, and she says, 'Well I'm not bothered about that, Shiraz! I don't mind criticism. I just take it on board and it makes me a stronger person! I won't let anyone bring me down!'

Just for a moment I felt hopeful when Carrie said that 'cos she looked so proper determined. Then she started singing 'Beautiful' by Christina Aguilera and it sounded a lot like when our Cava-Sue was giving birth to Fin. (The bit when Cava-Sue was mooing and screaming 'cos she could hardly push Fin's head out.) I can't honestly see folk paying ninety-nine pence to download that.

The rest of the night we were rooting through Carrie's walk-in wardrobe picking out dresses and bikinis and shoes for Ibiza. Carrie says I can lend what I like once we're there, which is well nice of her. Carrie chucked everything in a big pile and Maria's housekeeper lady Mrs

Raziq is going to wash and iron everything and pack Carrie's suitcase 'cos Carrie ain't good with stuff like that. Carrie is more spoiled now than she ever has been.

Anyway, after a while, Carrie forced me to confront my out-of-control-pube-problem. Carrie said, ''Ere, Shizzle, don't be a muppet! Remember I'm a trained beautician?! I've seen loads of folk's bits! You can't shock me!'

At first I says, 'No way.' Then Carrie says, 'Look, Shiz, the quicker you get 'em out, the quicker we can wax them off!' So I pulls down my trackie bottoms and Carrie stares for a while, and then she sighs proper LOUD and frowns. And then she says she'd try her best but she was thinking we might need a MUCH bigger box of strips. Cheeky cow. In the end Cazza got rid of most of them but it hurt like HELL. My fangita looks really weird now. It looks like when you pull Barbie's dress up and she's totally plastic smooth all the way round. Cava-Sue would be proper disappointed in me.

SUNDAY 6TH JUNE

2pm – TWO MORE SLEEPS UNTIL IBBBBBIZZZA!!!! Wooooooot woooot wooot wooooot!!!!

We just had a proper Wood family Sunday dinner. Nan came round and cooked. Mum, Dad, Nan, Clement, me, Cava-Sue, Lewis, Murphy and little Fin all crammed round the same table. It's not easy to do this now 'cos there's too many of us. We have to move the sofa and the coffee table, then carry the kitchen table through into the living-room and put up the extendable flap things on the table and even then Murphy has to sit on the arm of the couch eating on the corner. Murphy sulked right through dinner today anyway.

Murph says Sunday dinner just reminds him of his Ritu and how much she loved British stuff like roast spuds. Murph took a picture of his plate of grub on his phone and texted it to her in Osaka but she didn't text back and then he was so sad he couldn't eat anything else. All the while Cava-Sue was trying to eat her food with one hand with Fin on her lap who kept picking up peas and chucking them at Clement.

Anyway, have I mentioned that Nan's Sunday dinners are the best in the world. EVER! Even BETTER than when Carrie's dad takes Carrie and me to the Toby Carvery in Ilford where there is three types of meat and you can have unlimited roast potatoes and a 'bottomless' custard jug and they've got a *Who Wants To Be A Millionaire* machine that always seems to pay out the twenty quid. Toby Carvery is amazing. But Nan's cooking is proper AMAZING. I told Nan this today and she laughed and said that I'd 'made her day'. Mum looked well pissed off. This is 'cos last time Mum cooked Sunday lunch the chicken tasted of Cif Powergel cleaner and the gravy weren't even liquid, it looked like a poo in a jug and worst of all Lewis found what looked like a used elastoplast floating in his sweetcorn. BLEEEEEEEEUGH

– 'scuse me a moment while I stop writing and vom my brains out of my eyeholes bllagagaggggagaggah!

Mother spent most of today trying to put me off going to Ibiza. Mother says she's heard it's gonna chuck it down with rain all fortnight 'cos there are 'tropical storms' approaching the Balearic islands. Well, I had to laugh when she said that. 'Where did you hear that then, Mother?' I said.

Mum goes, 'Oooh, it was on that interwebby wotsit you and Murphy do.'

Now this is a bloody lie. Our mother can't use the internet and GOD KNOWS we've tried teaching her a thousand times. We get as far as showing her the Google home page and then she seems to have some sort of mentalist flip out and can't do the rest. In fact it's taken me and Murphy TWO WHOLE YEARS to show her how to set a reminder for herself on Sky Plus and even now when a message flashes up saying 'STARTS ON UK LIVING NOW' she gets all freaked out and starts shouting, 'Shiraz! What's it doing!!?? What's it doing? How does it know I like that!!? How!?'

Anyway, Mum reckons she was on the 'interweb' this morning and she read that the sea has been so choppy out in Ibiza that girls my age have been swept out to sea as far as Africa on inflatable lilos and eaten by crocodiles!

'Really, Mother?' I said trying to keep a straight face.

'I'm only saying what I saw,' she said. But even she couldn't keep her lips from twitching. Daft mare.

'Oooh, Shiraz,' Cava-Sue joined in. 'This severe weather is probably going to put the kaibosh on seeing an Ibiza sunset, yeah!' Then Cava-Sue had to explain to Mum all about Ibizan sunsets and how people say that you see one and it changes your life and broadens your horizons. Mum thought for a bit. She said she reckoned I probably wouldn't see no sunsets anyhow 'cos another thing wot she'd read on that interweb thing was that Ibiza was due for a plague of bees.

OH MY LIFE.

11.30pm – In fairness to my mother, I can sort of see why she's worried about me going away to Ibiza. She watched all them shows on Sky One full of girls acting like hoochies and getting arrested and chucking Es down their throat and snorting cocaine and weeing in the gutter. FOR CRYING OUT LOUD! I reckon telly is proper prejudicial and stigmatising towards young people. We don't ALL act like that.

I lived in London for almost a bloody year and the closest I got to being a hoochiemomma was that time at the House of Hardy grotto Christmas party where I had three large Tia Marias and got my boobs felt up by one of the other elves and even that time I told him to stop when the big lights came on at the end and I could see he'd got yellow spots round his nose and he'd vommed half-digested sausage roll down the front of his velour Santa's helper suit. Sometimes I wish I could just let go and be a hooch. I just can't. I am proper BORING. I'm not 'disruptive' and 'out of control' at all. Not like it used to say on my Year 8 and 9 reports from school.

Thing is, I can't say the same about some of the people in my class back at Mayflower. People like Kezia Marshall, bless her. I've just been round to see Kezia tonight and she ain't ever changing for NO ONE. Not even when she got knocked up by Luther Dinsdale. Or when Luther went in the navy and never had nothing to do with her no more. It's not like that made Kezia think, ''Ere better change my ways'. She won't never change her ways, that one. Kezia's still bare jokes and a bit mental. Like tonight, when I walked into Bargain Booze on the Woodbury Estate where she's working, she's like, 'Awwww, Shizzlebizzle, wa gwan? You put weight on your ass and your titties! And your waist is all small-little tiny! Ha ha ha! You look HOT innit! You'ze a top ranking bitch these days!' I gave Kezia a big hug. You just have to laugh at Kezia 'cos she says whatever she thinks and she don't mean no offence.

The way Kezia speaks is sort of a mix-up of accents. Kezia's mum Marlita is white and she's from Huddersfield and her real dad was white but she never knew him. But then Kezia's little sisters Desree and Patricia are mixed race 'cos her mother's next boyfriend Darryl was from Birmingham, but originally from Jamaica. So Kezia and her little sisters were looked after lots by Darryl's mum June, and June was proper Jamaican. June actually came here on a ship from Kingston Town, Jamaica, wearing a big hat, and her accent was proper strong.

So, Kezia is like pale white and ginger-haired, but she's also a bit black without being black at all. Thing is none of us in our class at Superchav Academy found that confusing at all 'cos that's just Kezia, innit. But some of the teachers found it annoying and they used to tell Kezia to 'speak properly and stop trying to be black'. They didn't understand that Kezia's whole family spoke like that! What was Kezia meant to bloody sound like? Princess bloody Eugenie?!! Grown-ups are proper small-minded sometimes. It well puts you off turning into one.

Looks-wise, though, Kezia has changed a bit since Mayflower. Before she had her baby, Kezia was small and quite curvy with boobs and a flat belly. But now she's got a bit of a wobbly belly and she's bigger all over on her arms and bum too. She still wears her big gold hoops and her charm bracelet but these days her hair is proper full on strawberry blonde with no blonde streaks or other colours in it to stop folk saying she's a ginger. Kezia's still good-looking though. She's got a cheeky face and lovely big blue eyes. Kezia was well popular with the boys at school. Maybe a bit too popular I reckon.

I wouldn't fancy working in that Bargain Booze one little bit. It is well rough. It's been robbed with guns twice this year. Kezia says she ain't bothered about getting robbed 'cos those knobhead fake-gangsters from the

Lark Drive Estate can just bloody have the till if they want it. It ain't nothing to her, is it? Kezia says if she gets taken hostage, well it'll be happy days 'cos the place is full of Irn Bru, WKD and Maltesers, so she'd be happier there than at home! Funny thing was that when I first walked into the shop tonight there was no one behind the counter at all. The till was standing there unguarded! So I bangs on the counter a bit and shouts 'Kezia!' and then I hears a bit of a clatter in the stock cupboard and then Kezia comes out looking a bit hot and bothered and then this bloke who looked about thirty walks out pretending to look at a clipboard saying, 'Mmmm, OK, Kezia, well it looks like all that stock is, erm, up to date! I'll inform head office!' and then he left as quick as he could. Well, when the door shut we both burst out laughing. I didn't ask Kezia what all that was about. I didn't wanna know. Then Rizalla who was taking over on the 7–11 shift showed up so Kezia grabs her hoodie and nicks us a tube of Pringles and two Twirls and a half litre of vodka and we set off to her flat on the third floor of Block D. On the way I asks Kezia how her little girl Latanoyatiqua Marshall-Dinsdale was keeping and she says, 'Oh yeah, Tiq's good s'pose, y'know. I mean, she's got this ear infection thingy at the moment so she's screaming all the time, but y'know I love her to bits, innit.'

Kezia says that her mum Marlita encouraged her to get a part-time job at Bargain Booze so Kezia could have some time outside the flat away from Tiq 'cos she was feeling proper stuck indoors 24/7. 'Thing is, Shizza, I do love Tiq. I wouldn't be without her. She's my little girl, innit?' Kez says to me. Well I just nods when she said this and said, 'Yeah I know, Kez,' but deep down I was thinking, 'Kez, but that's what girls always say about their babies don't they? 'Cos no one wants to give their own baby up once they've had it, but it doesn't mean you don't regret not using a condom and getting lumbered with one in the first place.' And I'm not being mean or nothing, but I totally reckon this is true. I'm only keeping it real.

So we gets back to Kezia's flat and Kezia's mother Marlita is in the living room with Tiq in her arms asleep, watching that film on Sky Movies where Jennifer Lopez is a wedding planner but she ain't exactly a good one 'cos she can't stop snogging the bloke she's meant to be organising a wedding for. Little Tiq looked like a proper angel lying there in Marlita's arms with her dummy in his mouth sound asleep. So Kez made us both a vodka and lemonade and eventually Tiq woke up and started to grumble a bit so Marlita took her off and changed her nappy and then gave her some Calpol for her ear and then puts her to bed, then Marlita comes in again and puts the baby monitor on the arm of her chair in case she woke up. Kezia is PROPER lucky having Marlita. Marlita's even going to take her holidays off work to look after Tiq when Kezia goes to Ibiza 'cos she wants Kezia to have some fun and not miss being young.

So I says to Kezia, ''Ere, do you think she'll miss you when you're away?!'

And Kezia says, 'Who?!'

And I says, 'Tiq!'

And Kezia thought for a second and says, 'Nah, she'll be OK. She loves being with her gran, don't she? 'Ere, Mum, Tiq called you Mama the other day didn't she?'

'Yeah,' nods Marlita. 'I reckon she was a bit confused.' I changed the subject then and talked about the holiday and sipped some of my vodka which was well too strong just like Kezia always used to make it in Year 9 when she'd show up at Goodmayes Park bandstand with some vodka nicked off her mum already mixed with Ribena in an old Pepsi bottle. And then Kezia made me look at her new bikini from TK Maxx. And all I can say is OH MY LIFE we won't be losing her on the beach in a hurry!! It's a Union Jack with BRITISH BABE written on the bum in sequins!!! Kezia's bikini is a lot tinier and brighter than one I would wear but Kezia was twirling about in it doing all sorts of model poses and pushing her boobs together like a Page 3 model! Kezia is proper confident about her body. She don't give a stuff what folk think about her. That's what makes her so much fun to be with.

And I'm lying in bed now thinking about the Union Jack bikini and I'm thinking that the best thing about it is that if I always lie beside Kezia on the beach, well honest to God, NO ONE is going to be looking at my pubes.

MONDAY 7TH JUNE

7pm – OH MY GOSH!! We fly at two o'clock tomorrow afternoon!! It's all happened so fast! I'm just sitting waiting for Uma to show up now with Zeus. Uma's staying over here tonight at Thundersley Road when she finishes her shift at Imperial Palace Casino. There's a Mahjong tournament tonight and she's one of the main croupiers!

When I chatted to Uma on MSN last night she was on the internet trying to learn little bits of Cantonese. NO REALLY. Uma says it's mostly old rich Chinese blokes who play Mahjong and that's how you make the biggest tips, just by being friendly and knowing the words for hello and thank you and all that. Uma is proper crafty like that. I reckon Uma's going to end up running her own casino one day. Whenever I say that my mother just goes, 'Pghghh!' Or, 'She'll end up in Holloway Prison for robbing one more like! At the end of the day, Shiraz, she's a Brunton-Fletcher! Jail's in their blood!'

That makes me really annoyed but I don't bother arguing with my mother about Uma. I'm just happy that Mum tolerates her now and seems to have forgiven her for that time in Year 7 when Uma stole one of her dad's dirty magazines and ripped it up and Pritt-sticked a page to the front door of every house in Thundersley Road.

In fairness Uma's dad WAS having an affair with some bird he met in his Alcoholics Anonymous meeting at the time and Uma was well jacked off with him. But that was ages ago. Uma's a lot better now. I asked her if she was going to pop in at Number 67 and see her mother Rose before she goes away, but Uma says no bloody way 'cos they're all doing her head in right now. Turns out Rose got caught trying to smuggle half a kilo of cannabis into Chelmsford Prison the other day for Clinton. Uma is bloody livid. She says she can't look at her right now.

Anyway, I'm looking forward to Uma getting here 'cos I need to tell her all my worries, especially what happened today. I just saw Wesley Barrington Bains II. My Wesley. Sitting outside Boots in the Ilford Xchange waiting for Sooz to finish work. Me and Carrie were in Boots getting some last minute bits for Ibiza and Carrie was going on and on and on to one of the assistants about which GHD gas cannisters to get that would last a whole fortnight 'cos she 'don't trust foreign electricity', so in the end I walked out 'cos I was well bored and that's when I saw him. He was sitting on a wall, sending a text, wearing his black New Era cap pulled down almost over his eyes and his dark green Nike hoodie all done up. He had on his pale blue fake Evisu jeans what I bought him for his last birthday and those Nike dunks he got in the sale at Lakeside when we went over last year to get Nan and Clement their wedding present. He looked lovely. Really lovely. Sort of tall with wide shoulders like a proper man, not a boy at all. And right then I remembered that he weren't there waiting for me he was waiting for Sooz.

And I felt all funny peculiar and weird and dizzy and a bit sick which is stupid 'cos we don't even go out no more which is totally my choice right?!! I ain't got any regrets about that!

The thing is, Wesley's gotta understand that I totally need space in my life to grow and work out who I am and who I want to be and where I'm coming from . . . and all sorts of other stuff that girls used to say on *The OC*, which seemed a good idea when I shouted them at Wesley back in April. Except the truth is I ain't had a sniff of male attention since then and now Wesley is in love with a miserable cow with an expression like she's permanently got sand in her vagina.

Anyway, Wesley sees me and his face all lights up. And he puts his phone away and he stands up to give me a hug but then he sort of stops himself and nudges my arm instead, then looks over my shoulder obviously checking if Sooz is coming. Well this sort of gives me the hump. 'Cos why should Sooz have a problem with me talking to Wesley? Why?! I knew him first! He's my friend and if she's got a problem she can go and spin on one for all I care. But I don't say this of course I say, 'Y'all right, Wes,' and he says, 'Y'all right, Shiz! Thought you were flying to Ibiza today, innit?!' So I smiles and says, 'Nah, tomorrow.' And then we stood looking at each other for a bit and I noticed a a bit of dried sleepdust on his cheek and I wanted to pick it off but I knew that it weren't really my place to do that any more.

So then Wesley told me this story about his mate Bezzie Kelleher who'd got headbutted down at Southend beach yesterday. Me and Wes were having a bit of a giggle about it to be honest 'cos AS USUAL it sounded like Bezzie was proper asking for a smack by being a bell-end and challenging strangers to rap battles. OMG Bezzie Kelleher is such a dick. Anyways me and Wes are laughing, but then suddenly Wesley stops laughing and I looks around and notices Sooz standing there. She was trying to smile but it was proper fake 'cos you could tell inside she was fuming. She had on that cropped Per Una burgundy jacket over her Boots uniform and a proper woman's brown leather handbag. I don't know where Sooz gets her clothes from. I reckon she's got a time tunnel to 1992 or something. And I'm not being horrible but her hair seemed to be having a hard time coping with the humidity 'cos it was a bit WOOOO-HAHHHH in parts like a magic troll. OK, I'll stop being a bitch now. Proper gospel truth about Sooz is that, no matter what she wears, she's got a pretty face and big boobs, so she always looks quite good. I wish she didn't but she does. She's prettier than me.

'All right, Sooz,' Wesley says to her, 'You know Shiraz, innit?'

Well Sooz just looks at me and goes, 'No. I've heard about you though. You were living in London weren't you?'

So I says, 'Mmm yeah, up until recently.'

Then Sooz says, 'Yeah, didn't my Wesley come through and see you when your sister went missing?'

Well, my heart nearly stopped then 'cos I didn't know that Sooz knew about Wesley coming to see me in London. I bloody hope she doesn't know that me and Wesley ended up snogging, either. And I mean PROPER snogging. Snogging with tongues against the door of my flat in Whitechapel. Wes sort of lifted me up by the waist and I wrapped my legs around his knee and we were both all breathless which was weird 'cos we weren't going out together any more. Then, about one day after that we decided we were TOTALLY NEVER EVER getting back together FOR EVER FULL STOP cos he was being all arsey about me going to Ibiza. SEE? This is totally why we can't be together 'cos he tries to get in the way of SHIRAZ BAILEY WOOD's journey as an individual.

'Erm yeah! London! Wes came to London to help me look for Cava-Sue,' I says to Sooz.

'Oh bless him!' Sooz says, proper patronising like he was a puppy or something, 'Aren't you soft, Wesley? You'll do anything for anyone won't you?'

Well this narked me a bit. I wanted to say, 'Well, thing is, Sooz, I ain't just ANYONE am I!? I know him better than anyone in the whole world. I know him better than you!' All the while Wesley wasn't really saying anything, his face was a bit red. Then Carrie walks up holding a big bag of Boots stuff and says, 'Oh all right, Wesley, wa gwan?' and Wes smiles and says, 'Aight, Cazza, been spending again, innit?' Then Sooz just stares at Carrie's pink mini skirt and flip flops and crop top like she's a bit of a hooch, so Carrie looks back at Sooz and wobbles her head a bit like a ghetto-ho and says to me, 'Damn, Shiz, that reminds me! HAIR CALMING SERUM. Knew I'd forgot something. Anyways . . . seeyas, both of you!' Then Carrie linked my arm and dragged me off whispering, 'Miserable cow, what's he doing with her?!' and then . . .

Ooh there's the front door. That'll be Uma.

2am – Bloody hell. I am proper squashed. I'm sharing my blow-up mattress with Uma and Zeus.

Our Penny is outside scratching the door and crying to get in and sniff Zeus's bum AGAIN. I'm not sure how much bum-sniffing Zeus will tolerate. Penny is proper unsubtle. Poor Uma was knackered when she turned up tonight. She's snoring her head off now. She turned up with FOUR HUNDRED QUID in a wodge of twenty quid notes in her pocket! Not bad for learning a few words of Cantonese, eh? She says she'll lend me some cash if things get tight for me in Ibiza. She is a proper star. I've took everything I own down Cash Converters now and I still ain't exactly rich.

I told Uma about me seeing Wesley earlier. Uma found it proper jokes when I told her about Carrie going all L'il Kim with Sooz. Then Uma stubs her Embassy Red out in her can of Cherry Coke, gives me one of her looks and says, 'Well, Shizzle, that one ain't over till it's over is it?'

So I says, 'What do you mean?'

Uma sighs and goes, 'Well I ain't seeing much closure on that one, innit?' Then she pulled the duvet over her and cuddled into Zeus and fell fast asleep!

What the hell is Uma bloody talking about? I'm proper OVER Welsey Barrington Bains II. I mean, yeah, I saw him today but it wasn't a big deal or nothing.

I've hardy even thought about it.

TUESDAY 8TH JUNE

7am!! OMMMMMMMMMG!!!!!

10am – IBBBBBBBBBBBBBIZZZZZZZZZZZZZZA!!!!!!

10.15am – Barney Draper driving us all to Heathrow in his Benz Jeep. We don't have to get the train! This day is just getting better and better!! We fly in four hours.

1pm – We're in Heathrow!! It is a bloody nightmare.

7pm – I don't bloody believe this! The thing is, I remember saying to Carrie when she booked those HappyFlight Airlines tickets, ' 'Ere, Carrie, these flights are a bit cheap, innit? Ain't that the holiday company who are always on *Watchdog* on BBC1? They're a right bunch of crooks aren't they? Aren't they always cancelling planes?! We're not going to end up kipping overnight in Heathrow Airport are we?!'

Well, Carrie got the hump when I said that and she says, ' 'Ere, Shiz, why you always got to be such a stress head?' And I goes, 'I'm just saying that the flights seem very cheap!' Then Carrie says, 'Of course the flights are cheap! Flights have got to be well cheap these days! HappyFlights NEED customers now that all those hippytreehugger types are making folk feel so guilty about carbon bloody feetmarkthings, innit? Those bloody hippies want us all to stay indoors and only go on our holibobs to places we can walk to! They want us in teepees knitting our own yoghurt and wearing tie-dye vests and self-cleaning knickers!' Carrie stopped ranting then 'cos she knew she was dissing my Cava-Sue who has just bought herself a pair of self-cleaning knickers from the stop-the-pollution.com website.

'So you think the flights will be OK then?' I says again. I couldn't say too much really 'cos after all it was Carrie's dad who had paid for the flights. It was his little present to Carrie to help her get over the trauma of college, and I'm coming to keep an eye on her.

'Look, don't worry about HappyFlights, Shiz! It'll be fine!' says Carrie. Fine? Here we all are sat in bloody Sunshine Sandwiches in Heathrow waiting for our flight – which is now FIVE HOURS LATE ALREADY – to be called, with no clue as to when it might go!! In fact, the last time Uma went and hassled one of the HappyFlight bods he said he wasn't exactly sure when Flight A107 to Ibiza might depart. He said they weren't sure where the

41

plane even was or the pilot either!! HOW DO YOU LOSE A PLANE!!!!????

10pm – Still no news on the plane. We're now EIGHT hours late.

We just sent Kezia to hassle the bod on the desk again. Kezia seems to get answers much quicker than all of us. Maybe that's 'cos she's small and tough, and she's wearing a bright yellow green and black Jamaica football team tracksuit over a Union Jack bikini with a rave whistle round her neck, that she sometimes blows when she gets impatient. Kezia can get a bit lairy sometimes. Kezia's just bought a bottle of Jamaican rum from Duty Free to drink on the flight and good job Uma's talked her out of opening it. Uma says we already made a big enough scene at the check-in desk so we should keep it on the low for a while till we get to the other end.

The check-in drama wasn't Kezia's fault. It was Carrie being a ditz. Basically we were all in the queue waiting to check-in our suitcases and this stern looking woman asked Carrie if anyone had 'helped her pack her suitcase' or given her 'anything to carry' and Carrie says 'Yeah, course. I never packed my suitcase at all! Mrs Raziq did it!' So stern woman goes, 'Who is Mrs Raziq? Where is she from?' And Carrie goes, 'I dunno. She's from Pakistan or Afghanistan or somewhere! What's your problem? She gave me some food to bring with me too! It's in that box there look!'

Well then things went a bit mental. First an alarm

began screaming WAH WAH WAH WAH and then some blokes in police uniforms carrying machine guns arrived and then some other blokes with walkie-talkies arrived and they're all crowding around Carrie asking her stuff and threatening to blow up her suitcase!! Well Carrie's going off her nut then, shouting, 'Oi matey! Are you mental? Don't you blow up my suitcase! There's two pairs of Christian Louboutin stilettos in there! They ain't fakes off Walthamstow market or nothing! They're real! Why you all up in my face? I ain't done nothing!'

Then the machine gun men start asking about the 'food' Cazza had been 'asked to carry' acting like it's a bomb or some explosives or something! So Carrie flips open her suitcase and gets out a tupperware box and shouts, 'Oh bloody hell! They're bloody pakoras! Have them! I only brought them 'cos Mrs R was nagging me to eat proper in Ibiza 'cos I'll never find a husband being so skinny!' So then one of the blokes with a gun helps himself to a pakora and tastes one and then another security guard ate one too and then everyone seemed to calm down lots and the police agreed that they were 'very tasty' but they'd still need to confiscate the box 'for further investigation'. And then they let Carrie go.

But by this point it was almost two o'clock so we all had to run as fast as we could, knocking people to the side and tripping over kids and believe me this would have been FAR LESS STRESSFUL if we'd known some knobhead had lost the plane and the pilot was still in bloody bed and we were trapped in Heathrow Terminal 1 FOR EVER!!!

11pm – I think Uma's nicotine withdrawal is starting to kick in. She ain't had an Embassy Red since 1.30pm this afternoon. Uma says the only place you can smoke in Heathrow is a broom cupboard in Terminal 4 and that's almost three miles away and you have to share the cupboard with six other folk with yellow hands all coughing up bits of their lungs into the cleaner's mop bucket. Uma says it is MINGING. Uma says she's fine to go without a fag, in fact it'll be good for her.

11.25pm – Oh God. Uma says she's gasping for a fag so much that her gums feel itchy, and she says she can feel hair sprouting on the back of her hands.

11.40pm – Uma is rocking backwards and forwards in her seat and biting her fingernails. I think she's beginning to crack.

11.45pm – Uma has just told Kezia that if she blows that bloody whistle one more time and shouts 'Goodmayes Girls Run Ting!!' she's going to rip it off and stuff it into an, erm, very intimate part of Kezia's downstairs region.

12pm – OH NO. Uma's just been over to the HappyFlights desk and shouted at the bloke to give her a plane 'cos she'll fly it there her sodding self.

12.05am – I've just asked Carrie to take Uma to Terminal 4 to the cancer broom cupboard for a ciggie. I told Carrie to make sure Uma smokes at least three and applies some fresh Nicotine patches too.

1am – OH THANK GOD!!! We're being called to Gate 79 for our flight to Ibiza. The bods say the gate is about half a mile away but there's loads of those travelator moving walkways on the way!!! I love them walkways things!! I can do amazing breakdancing on them. Hooray! We're on our way!! Ibiza here we come!!! Woooooot woooot!!! B to the R to the A to the P!!!!!!!

1.35pm – Bollocks.

2.35am – Well this is a RIGHT OLD SHAMBLES. Nicky Campbell on *Watchdog* is well going to be hearing about this. We still haven't got a pilot to fly us to Ibiza!! We've only been moved to Gate 79 'cos that's where we'll be flying from 'eventually'. OMG I am so pissed off. Gate 79 is the most bloody boring place in the world. It's just a big white room full of people who should be in Ibiza all scowling at each other and occasionally doing silent but violent farts then not fessing up to it. I AM IN HELL. BABY JESUS WHY ARE YOU PUNISHING ME? WHY??

2.45pm – Kezia has opened her rum and is passing it around. I'm bloody having a big gulp.

3am – Kezia is encouraging everyone at Gate 79 to open their Duty Free booze and 'make some noize'.

3.15am – OH MY DAYZ. Why does it always take booze to make things better!? Everybody was proper scowling at each other half an hour back and now everyone is laughing and swapping mobile phone numbers and talking about what clubs we're all going to and flirting with each other too! This is too jokes. Kezia and Uma are now sat in the middle of a gang of lads from Catford. They're about our age. I think one of them is called Taz and another is called Leon. They're all quite buff actually. Not that I'm perving or nothing. Leon has just made a big point of telling us that they're all totally single. Kezia actually yelped with excitement.

3.30am – Carrie's just come back from chatting up some blokes from Kent who must be, like, twenty-seven or something. They were a lot older than us anyway. Carrie says the one she likes best is called Frankie and said he's a DJ. Carrie says Frankie can get us into the Hard2Beat night at Pacha for FREE! Carrie says Frankie's mates all work in the 'entertainment industry' so they fly back and forth to Ibiza all the time so he knows the island like the back of his hand. Carrie says Frankie is proper gorgeous and just her type. Frankie and Carrie have swapped mobile phone numbers already. Here we go again.

3.45am – Oh no. Uma has just suggested to the Catford boys – Taz, Leon, Davo and Tyrone – that they might like a quick game of poker for MONEY. Uma says she's not amazing at poker but it'll pass the time. Uma is lying. This isn't going to be pretty. Last time I saw Uma do this at a party she kept on playing until one bloke lost £500, his Rolex and his trainers. Uma, I LOVE U darling but U iz a hustler.

4am – Uma should really give Taz from Catford his

Ralph Lauren jersey back. I mean, yeah he lost it fair and square but he's a nice lad and he's going to be cold on the plane. Uma mate, HAVE A HEART!

4.15am – Uma has relented and given Taz his jersey and Evisu jeans back. THANK GOD.

5am – THE PILOT IS HERE! WE'RE LEAVING IN THIRTY MINUTES. Hosannah! I was starting to feel proper anxious again, but then this geezer in a HappyFlights pilot uniform just walked past. He looked well knackered 'cos he'd just flown a plane from Antwerp, but he's agreed to fly us to Ibiza! I just heard him tell the other crew he could do with the extra money! He says it's a proper easy route so he can put it on auto-pilot and have a snooze. What a nice bloke!

5.05am – I hope he was kidding about the snooze bit.

5.30am – We're on the plane. We're about to go. Ibiza here we come!! NO REALLY THIS TIME. Woot wooot woooootage!

WEDNESDAY 9TH JUNE

6pm – Apartments La Paradiso. San Antonio, Ibiza.

We're here! And the weather is totally roasting hot sunny! I just rang Sean and Danny to tell them and they were so jealous 'cos they don't fly till Sunday morning! And our apartment is proper swish, all white marble with a good shower and everything! We're on the third floor with a balcony overlooking the pool! And the pool has its own DJ and there are loads of well buff boys in trunks sitting around it. And not that many girls – HA HA HA! I reckon there's four boys to every one girl. Even Kezia, who ain't exactly Albert Einstein, worked that one out in five seconds.

We didn't get to Ibiza until about one o'clock this afternoon, so we've all been lying in our beds for a few hours recovering. It is AMAZING to have a proper bed, even if mine is right beside Kezia's and she sleeps with no knickers on and keeps pulling her sheets off and I'm so close I can see all the smudged letters of the GOODMAYES 4 LIFE tattoo on her bum. Never mind though, I AM SO HAPPY TO BE HERE.

6.45pm – Uma and Kezia have just got back from the 'supermercado'. Ha! See I am speaking Spanish! We each put in twenty euros to get some supplies. Uma got us bread, milk, bananas, eggs, beans, marmite, loo roll, water, crisps and a massive box of Honey Nut Loops. Kezia bought twelve Smirnoff Ices, two bottles of Peach Lambrini and a big bag of Revels. Kezia says the Revels are to line her stomach. She has already drunk two of the Smirnoff Ices.

7.15pm – Our holiday rep bod Billy has just knocked on our door to say hello. We're invited to an Official Welcome Meeting at eleven tomorrow morning in the downstairs bar! Billy is tall with dyed blonde hair and tanned skin and he's quite good-looking (which he totally knows) and he's a proper flirt. Carrie nearly shoved an orange Revel in her lughole by accident when he walked in. Billy had on a red jacket with HappyFlight Holidays written on the chest and white shorts which could do with being less short IF YOU KNOW WHAT I MEAN.

Anyway he just walks in and sees us all looking like sweaty biffers eating our Revels and Honey Nut Loops and he says, totally like he meant it, 'Oh my gosh, I feel like I've died and gone to heaven . . . unless these are earth angels I see before me.' Well Uma put her head under the table and made a fake chucking up sound, but Carrie went, 'Heeheeeheeeheeehee!!!' Then she snorted Smirnoff Ice down her nostrils.

Billy said, 'So will I be seeing you at the Welcome Meeting?' And Kezia says, 'Well I dunno, can we start it a bit later than eleven 'cos I'm planning on getting well hammered tonight, bruv?'

Well, Billy just looked at Kezia – who was rubbing Cocoa Butter into her boob stretch marks – and he wrinkled his nose a bit and said, 'Sorry, no.'

So he's gone now and us 'earth angels' have decided to go for some drinks. We're just off to the bars downstairs tonight, 'cos we don't really have a clue where we are. It's not going to be a big night, I don't reckon. We've got plenty of time for that. I'll only have a couple I think.

1.20am – dearrrsiary ooohh hang on nooo. Kezzzzia no youcan't look!!! This is my privatdiary!!!!

1.27am – dere diary tonight wuz hilareous cuz

1.30am – Deer deiary.

It probabaly ain't a good ideea to try and write my thoughts when I've bin drinking but I want to get it down on record fur WHEN I writ my future autobiography that tonight wuz bare jokes and LULZ and Roflcopter and LOLERSKATES and all that sort of shizzam, innit. And I'm thinkin that maybe WAS a BIG NITE OUT 'cos we are all well squiffy and sadly now we can't never go back to The Lucky Shamrock bar 'cos Kezia got proper overexcited when they played her favourite Cascada song and she lay on the bar and got some random lads from Cardiff to drink shots of Baileys out of her bellybutton with a straw and then we got chucked out which is quite bad innit THEENDGOODNITEFANKUGOODMAYES GIRLSRUNTING!XX

THURSDAY 10TH JUNE

10am – Oh God no. My head is killing me.

10.15am – Ooh poor Kezia. She is proper sick.

10.30am – I dunno how Kez has got anything left inside her. She must have spewed ten times.

10.45am – Kezia says she ain't coming to the rep's Meeting. Kezia reckons she's on the mend though 'cos she's at the white foam stage of spewing and there's no more Revels coming out. Kezia says she wants to stay clinging to the toilet 'cos it's the only thing in this bloody stupid country that's cold.

10.55am – Me, Carrie and Uma are off to the Welcome Meeting. Carrie has been GHDing her hair for an hour and rubbing factor 30 sun shimmer into her shoulders. Carrie ain't got a hangover 'cos she drank a glass of water after every one of booze and had a massive bowl of Honey Nut Loops to line her stomach before she went out. Carrie said she has to take it easy with the booze as she wants to 'protect her voice'.

Uma said Carrie don't need anything to protect her voice, it's the rest of us that needs protecting 'cos it already sounds like a bloody burglar alarm.

Carrie laughed at that, but not very loudly.

8pm – Well, there's a shock. I didn't think that the Welcome Meeting would be jokes but it sort of was. There are some proper funny people in this apartment block. I may as well write this down 'cos I'm having last turn in the shower tonight and we're still waiting for Carrie to exfoliate her knees. So anyways, me, Uma and Carrie went to the bar today to be 'officially welcomed' by Billy. There was about thirty people there, including all the Catford boys, Taz, Leon, Davo and Tyrone. They all looked a bit battered 'cos they'd had a big night out last night too. Taz was drinking a black coffee with his sunglasses on looking a bit shaky so I says, 'Too sunny for you in here, is it?' and he laughed and said, 'Oh, I fell asleep with my contact lenses in last night. My eyes are killing me.' So I giggles and tells him about us all in The Lucky Shamrock and he was laughing and he says, 'The thing is, that was my first night on the booze for weeks too, 'cos I been working right up 'till we flew.'

So I says, 'Oh right, what do you do?'

And he goes, 'Oh, I'm a fireman.'

Well, obviously, after he said that I couldn't actually speak for a while as I was imagining Taz in his uniform, 'cos I've got to admit that the Fire Brigade must be properly my favourite emergency service ever. In fact, that time Uma burned Mayflower Academy assembly hall down during the Winter Festival by setting light to the festive paperchains with an aerosol and a lighter, well I was proper narked at her but we did have a lovely time outside sitting on the wall watching Goodmayes Fire Brigade all sweating and wrestling with their massive hoses. That was A-MAZING. So anyway, I tried to sit down beside Taz but Carrie jumps into my seat and says, 'OOOh, Taz, you're a fireman!? How brave is that? What a hero!' And I'm left sitting beside his mate Davo who is nice looking and that but he's got a weird laugh and he's only about one and a half metres tall and I don't reckon he's a fireman at all, 'cos if he is it must be at BLOODY LEGOLAND.

Anyway, there was loads of other boys and girls at the meeting who looked like a good laugh. There was a group of girls from Dorset who all had the same haircut and a group of lads from Bristol and a big mixed group from Rhyl in Wales who all worked at the same factory. It was funny 'cos everyone was about our age except this old couple of dears called Mavis and Wilf who were sitting on the front row in cardigans and shorts and sunhats and socks over sandals, both wearing bumbags. They must have been about seventy! So Taz says to Wilf and Mavis how come they ended up in San Antonio, Ibiza? And Wilf says he ain't got a clue, it's Mavis who always goes on the Teletext looking for bargains and she's a bit blind and she can't read stuff properly.

Well we all laughed when he said that and then Mavis says, 'Oh well, never mind, it keeps life exciting.' And then she said that so far they've met nothing but lovely young people who've been proper polite. Then Wilf says, 'Well aside from this ginger lass with tattoos who they had to tell to shut up last night 'cos she was outside their window at 3am shouting at dustbins and challenging passers-by to press-up competitions.' Well, everyone was howling when Wilf said that aside from me, Carrie and Uma who all stared at our flip flops.

Well, then Billy flounces in, wearing his everyone-please-look-at-my-trouser-salami shorts, holding his clipboard and he shouts, 'Are we all having a happy holiday?! Say, "Yes Billy!"'

And everyone shouts, 'Yes!' aside from Uma who has taken a dislike to Billy on account of him being a 'greasy false git', so she just pulled the same face she used to do to the Truancy Officer when he used to sneak up behind her in Claire's Accessories and totally ruin her afternoon of stealing hoop earrings.

So then Billy rattles proper quickly through some vital information about San Antonio, like how it is very hot so we'd better put sun cream on and we might get thirsty so we better drink water and how it's not a good idea to give cheek to policemen here 'cos they're not like cops in Britain and they won't be all soft and give you a dispersal order, they will batter you with truncheons and you ain't got no human rights. Then Billy told us we'll never be getting hungry in San Antonio 'cos you can get chips and burgers EVERYWHERE.

And that was sort of that. Then he said, 'Any questions?' and I asked if there was an internet café near by, but Billy gave me well complicated directions to the nearest one, which was a pain 'cos I've told our Murphy he should mail me if he's feeling crap and I'd write back. I hope I find it, wherever it is, 'cos I need to update my Bebo with pics of me snogging bare choong boys to prove to Wesley I am well over him now, which I totally ain't.

Then Carrie puts her hand up and goes, 'Erm, Billy, I thought you might have some info on clubs and DJs and secret beach parties. Like, which clubs have carry-on parties during the day and all that?' Well Billy just seemed to be a bit deaf when she said that. So Carrie says, 'Do you know what night the All Around the World party is on at Amnesia? Where do we get those flyers so the tickets are half price? Well Billy just smiled then and told us that she didn't need to worry about clubs 'cos he had some AMAZING EXCURSIONS AND TRIPS that we should book off him TODAY.

For example, did we know there is a Parrot Park on the island with parrots that can do amazing tricks like ride little bikes and say rude words? The ticket is one hundred euros for the day and for that you drink unlimited vodka and get your photo taken with the parrot on your head too!? Well no one sounded proper thrilled by that trip at all.

Billy said he was running a trip to a botanical gardens on the other side of the island. The coach picks you up at 8am and you can travel through stunning scenery on the way for only eighty-eight euros, which includes a free kebab and a can of Stella Artois when you get there. Well no one went for that either. So then Billy says he had a trip that we would be TOTALLY MENTAL not to book and that was the official HappyFlight Holidays Booze Cruise tomorrow afternoon which is only seventy-five euros and it is AN INCREDIBLE DAY OUT. About three hundred people go on a special boat with a glass bottom and there's a DJ on board and unlimited drink and dancing and swimming and snorkling and games and all sorts of adventures!! And the booze cruise is the best ever way to see an Ibizan sunset 'cos you are literally on a boat facing it and it will be the most amazing day of your life ever. But we had to book straight away NOW this moment as he only had thirty tickets left and was just off to do another welcome meeting in Playa Del Bossa and everyone there was dying to go too!

Well Carrie looks proper excited then. And so did Taz and Leon and Davo and even Uma did a bit and then everyone started saying, 'OK then, I'll have a ticket!' and we were all chucking euros at Billy including old Wilf who got told to sit down by Mavis 'cos he wasn't going, no way, not after what happened that time in Jamaica when he ended up in the medical room for three days after limbo dancing.

So, anyway, we bought four tickets for the Goodmayes Girls to go on the booze cruise! And then we all got into our bikinis, went to the pool and we lay in the sun and got a bit brown and Uma was on proper hilarious form doing her David Blaine card tricks to entertain all the Rhyl crew and Carrie was being a usual man magnet with her teeny-weeny lemon bikini and Kezia was pretty quiet and sleepy and no trouble and there wasn't a cloud in the sky and I didn't feel too paranoid in my bikini, in fact I felt OK and not like Upsy-Daisy and I never thought about any of my problems like Wesley or Murph or my destiny or anything like that, I just had a good laugh.

In fact, to be honest, I'm having the best time of my life ever.

FRIDAY 11TH JUNE

8.30am – Internet café. Got an email from Murph this morning.

From – murphdog92@widebleyonder.com
To – theshizzlebizzle@hotmail.com

Aight shiz, wa gwan sis? Hope u iz avin a bare jokes holiday. Iz it well hot? Wots Ibiza like? Saw *Uncensored Ibiza* on Bravo last night and it looked well gud. There was this one bird innit with well big knockers dancing on a table and the table bust and she lands on the floor nearly squashing this other geezer. I was laffing at that. I ain't been laffin that much this week really. I feel well mental right now. Fing is Shizzle, evah since Ritu went home I don't see anyfing much in this shit world to laff at. Honest Shiz, my head is proper bended with it all coz I reckon she has forgot me. And I totally knows it that me and her are well supposed to be together. Don't ask me how I know, I just know. Fing is Shiz you says to me I should tell you how I feel and not bottle it all up and that iz how I feel, like sad but mostly proper angry coz I love Ritu, I love the way she iz and how she meks me luk at life an

Personalise your messages at widebleyonder with smiles!
Go to www.smileyfactory-wby.com and make your mails miles better!

8.45am – Internet café. Another email from Murph.

From – murphdog92@wideblueyonder.com
To – theshizzlebizzle@hotmail.com

Aight Shiz. Wa gwan?

  Shiz. This is important. I was just writing you this email right and I was reading back what I'd said and to be honest it was well gay so I wasn't going to send it but then bloody Zeus jumped up and knocked the keyboard and I dunno if it was sent or not coz it ain't in the sent box. But if it was sent DON'T read it coz I never meant none of it. PLEASE. And I gotta go now coz me and Sizzle and Tariq are walking to school togever coz we gotta roll deep these days coz Thundersley Road Man Dem needs to represent wot with us having to walk through Lark Rise Estate which is dangerous these days wot with so many soldiers on the street willin to die. Big tings are gwan, sista. Murphdogxx

Personalise your messages at wideblueyonder with smiles! Go to www.smileyfactory-wby.com and make your mails miles better!

10pm – I may as well write this now, 'cos I'm not sure how long we might be waiting. You never know in these places do you? Today has been a proper adventure. I might's well start from the beginning 'cos it looks like there's a bit of a queue so I got plenty time. Besides, when they make a film of my life one day the director bloke will need loads of detail.

So basically, we all woke up this morning really early 'cos the sun was shining really brightly into the apartment. Oh and Kezia was chucking up again. And all the time Kez was in the loo, her phone was bleeping like mad. So in the end I picks it up and there's a text message flashing from her mother Marlita. Well I panics a bit 'cos I thought it might be an emergency with Tiq or something so I opened it and I wish I didn't now 'cos it was a picture of Tiq smiling in her cot with a message under it obviously typed by Marlita saying 'I MISS YOU MUMMY! WRITE ME A TEXT!' so I stared at that and then another message bleeped from Marlita and this time it was a text saying, 'Kezia, just to say that we are all doing good here. Tiq is fine. But we would appreciate a phone call or something to know you are alive. Love Mum xxx'

Well I went into the bathroom and fessed up what I saw right away 'cos I didn't want Kezia to think I was being sneaky. But Kezia wasn't upset or nothing. She just said, 'Oh, OK, I'll text them tonight or something, thanks babe.' Then she washed her face and put on her Union Jack bikini and had a piece of bread with marmite on it and said she felt much better and she didn't know why she's feeling so crap 'cos she was only drinking single gin and Yakults last night and those Yakult things are supposed to be a health thing, innit?

Well, I told Uma about the text message when we were on the coach to where the booze cruise set off from. Uma whispered to me she reckons Kezia is just trying to block home out of her head 'cos she's been finding being a mum proper hard, living up all those flights of stairs on the Woodbury Estate. It's hard work just to take the pram anywhere. Uma was saying that Uma's brother Clinton who always fancied Kezia even stole Kezia a Bugaboo Cameleon Pram from Mothercare so she'd be able to get out and about a bit easier. Well we both stopped gossiping then 'cos Billy Big Gob our holiday rep had hold of the microphone and was shouting, 'Are we all having a Happy Holiday!? Say, "Yes we are Billy!"' And everyone shouted, 'Yes we are Billy!' and then he told us that today was going to be a day we would remember for the rest of our lives and how once we got on the boat we could leave all our cares behind. Then he said how all the booze on the boat was free and we should drink as much as possible and 'go mental'. Everyone cheered when he said that aside from Uma who don't really do cheering and shouting things to order.

Then Billy asked if we had any questions and I felt like asking if he had any plans in the near future to buy bigger shorts 'cos if I got one more glimpse of 'Little Billy' hanging out of the side of those things, well my Honey Nut Loops were gonna be making a return appearance. OMG it is well minging. It reminds me of Year 7 science when we put this formaldehyde stuff on a patch of soil and watch all the worms coming gasping to the surface for air. BLOODY DISGUSTING. Well I told Taz and Leon that and they were howling laughing. Taz looks lovely when he laughs 'cos he's got amazing brown eyes and they sort of twinkle. And the thing is . . . I think he might fancy me a little bit! I ain't one hundred per cent sure, but if he does it will be AMAZING 'cos he's proper beautiful and he's got a well buff body with muscles and a six-pack and he's got dark brown hair that goes all over his head NOT like my Wesley who has a patch missing on the top. Poor Wes's hair looks a bit like it's been coloured in by a small child who sort of got bored three-quarters of the way through and walked off.

The thing about Taz is that he is a FIREMAN. Did I write that before? HE IS A FIREMAN! He saves people's lives and wears a uniform and can carry people over his shoulder.

Well anyway, when we were on the coach today Taz said I was the funniest girl he's met for ages. Taz says it's lovely to meet a girl who is so funny and so pretty too. So I says to Taz, that's a shame 'cos I was just thinking how boring and butterz he was. Well Taz nearly wet himself laughing when I said that and called me a cheeky mare. That's the weird thing about some boys, the ruder you are to them the more they like you. Then we got off the coach and got on the boat and Carrie says to me, ' 'Ere, Shiz, do you fancy Taz?' So I says, 'Erm nah, I mean, I dunno.' So Carrie says, 'Oh good, 'cos I'm not being funny or nuffin but I think he's after me anyway. He's always looking at my boobs.' So I says, 'Well in fairness Carrie everyone's looking at your boobs. You've got a push-up bikini that lifts them so high they're either side of your ears, WE AIN'T GOT NO CHOICE.' But then Kezia came over with a round of shots called Slippery Nipples which we all downed in one and shouted, 'Goodmayes Girls Run Ting!' and then some other girl was running round with a watering-can full of vodka and Redbull pouring it into everyone's mouths and the DJ started playing a set which was mostly big bassline tracks that everyone knew so everyone was dancing and the boat sailed out of the harbour and into the middle of nowhere and there wasn't a cloud in the sky and all the girls were dancing in bikinis and the boys with no tops on and sunglasses. It looked like a Beyoncé video or something!

Then things started to get really messy 'cos everyone was chucking back booze and getting totally hammered. OK, everyone aside from me and Uma. Uma isn't really a big drinker any more. Not that she ever bangs on about it or tries to stop anyone else having fun. You'd never really notice. Uma sort of stopped drinking after Year 11 when her dad went back in Alcoholics Anonymous and Uma went to Portsmouth to see him and he was promising to stop the drinking but he didn't. The next thing we hear he'd been arrested for punching his girlfriend Mica when he was pissed and she chucked him out and he was living rough. Then he went back in prison for some burglary he did when he'd had a bottle of Scotch. Drinking is a proper funny thing, isn't it? It can make you the happiest person in the whole world but if you start liking it too much you can ruin your life. I was thinking about all of this when I was watching Kez being all drunk and lairy and half snogging with one lad and then forgetting about him on the way to the bar and proper slow windin' with another one. Booze makes people forget all about real life. But just for a bit, like they've put it on Sky Plus pause. Except the thing is real life is always going to be waiting for you once you've sobered up and . . . OH MY DAYZ, listen to me?! I sound like I'm thirty-five or something, cheer up, Shiraz, you boring cow. LMAO!

I think I'm being all bloody Sonia-Cathcart-I-wear-a-Jesus-Christ-Is-Everywhere-bumbag-and-I'm-going-to-heaven-and-you-ain't about booze 'cos of what happened next. So Carrie, who was 'protecting her singing voice' today by chucking back one Bacardi and Banana Nesquik after another and smoking Marlboro Lights when she don't even smoke, was being the life and soul of the party. She was first up playing spin the bottle when a game was getting organised AND SHE GOT TO KISS TAZ (the cow), then she won the Dirty Dancing competition by managing to hook both ankles over some poor bloke's shoulders and getting him to swing her round and round to a track by Scooter. OH, AND YES I FILMED ALL THIS

ON MY CAMERA BY THE WAY, CARRIE, AND YOU BETTER BE NICE TO ME 'COS IT MIGHT ACCIDENTALLY END UP ON BEBO!!!!

Well, after that Carrie was showing some of the boys from Rhyl how she could do the splits like a proper Olympic athlete. And then she started singing really loudly to show everyone she was a 'trained singer'. Then she started singing the theme song from that old film *Titanic* what's always on at Christmas – 'My Heart Will Go On' by that Celine Dion bird. The one with the sinking boat. And then Carrie screams, 'Ooh this is like *Titanic* ain't it!? Look! Look I'm like that woman on *Titanic*!' Then Carrie ran to the side of the boat and sort of climbed up on the railings and put her hands out and shouted, 'I'm the King of the World! Listen everyone! I'm the King of the World.' And then one of her flip flops fell off into the sea and the last words I heard her say were, 'Ooh, my flip flop! Oh bloody hell! They're from Mango too. I had to order them online . . . oooooh noooooo aaaaaaaaaaagh . . .' And then she disappeared! Over the side of the boat. CARRIE FELL IN THE SEA!!! Well luckily me and Uma saw it happen 'cos everyone else was too drunk to notice and I was screaming at the blokes who were driving the boat, 'She's fell in! She's fell in!'

Well, all hell let loose then 'cos it's not like Carrie was wearing a life-jacket or anything and she was really drunk. So they stopped the boat and thank GOD we could see her flapping about around two hundred metres back. I knew Carrie could swim a bit but not that brilliant 'cos she always used to skip swimming lessons in Year 8 at Mayflower 'cos she had hair extensions and she didn't want them to go green.

So, they turned the boat around really quickly and sailed back to where Carrie was and then some lad called Squiggy from Stockport totally seemed to take control of the situation and he shouts, 'It's OK I'll get her. I'm a lifeguard.' Then he dived in and saved her and swam her back to the boat with his arm cupped around her neck, swimming on his back. Two other blokes pulled her over the railings. Carrie was really crying. She said she thought she was going to die. I was crying a bit too to be honest 'cos I thought for a moment I'd never see her again. Oh, I don't even want to think that. She's been my bezzie for ever and I'd go crazy if anything happened to her.

So anyway, Carrie wasn't really hurt or nothing, but the captain said we should take her to the hospital for a check-up 'cos where she fell in was around a raw sewage pipe and the sea is proper disgusting. Carrie said she felt OK and she couldn't be bothered so I pointed out to her that she had bits of wet loo roll in the back of her hair and that's how we ended up here in the emergency room in San Antonio Hospital getting ignored by all these nurses who look really pissed off with us and keep pretending not to speak English. And Kezia doesn't understand they're just pretending so she just keeps shouting, 'OI, HOMBRE! DON'T YOU SPEAK ENGLISH? OUR FRIEND AIN'T WELL! COMPRONDO?' proper loudly at them. And we've been here for five hours now and come to think about it, if some film director does make a movie of my life, this hospital bit would be the boring bit where you could go for a wee 'cos this is BLOODY CRAP.

Midnight – Just remembered. Never saw the sunset. I was too busy watching Carrie doing the doggy paddle in raw sewage. Not really the same thing is it?

SATURDAY 12TH JUNE

11am – Carrie is really enjoying all the fuss she's getting around our apartment block about the booze cruise accident. The story gets worse every time I hear it! Wilf and Mavis heard off the bloke in the supermercado that Carrie was pushed off the boat by a maniac and she had to swim to the nearby island of Formentera where she was picked up by a police helicopter! They seemed sort of disappointed when I said that weren't true.

Carrie says she feels like a celebrity today on account of her falling off the boat yesterday. This doesn't surprise me at all. Carrie loves being in the spotlight. She's a bit addicted to it. For example, and this is really BAD, last year I switched on *Sky News* and there was this story about a boy called Dwayne getting shot dead in Plumstead and all the news teams were down there filming his mates leaving flowers and baseball caps and drawings and all that and it was proper sad 'cos he was only about fifteen and his mates were crying their eyes out and giving little interviews about how great he was and then in the background of the shot I couldn't believe what I was seeing. It was Carrie Draper! Carrie Draper bawling her eyes out, tying flowers to a lamppost. The camera was on her for ages too 'cos she had hotpants on! CARRIE DIDN'T EVEN KNOW DWAYNE.

So I rings Carrie's mobile and live on the screen in front of me I could see her pick it up so I goes, ''Ere, Carrie, why are you in Plumstead crying over a boy you ain't never met!?'

So Carrie says, 'Oh hiya, Shiz. Well Chantalle Strong was coming over here 'cos it's her mum's friend's next-door neighbour's son, so I thought I'd come too. 'Ere, Shiz it's proper emotional! I'm going to give a little interview on *News 24* in a moment! What does my hair look like?!'

THAT IS HOW MUCH CARRIE LOVES BEING IN THE SPOTLIGHT.

This would be bare jokes if it weren't so sick. Actually it's still bare jokes. Carrie Draper just is bare jokes. I'm so glad she's alive and well and the hospital gave her the all-clear. They say she's fine although they wouldn't advise her to go swimming around again in used tampons and bog roll for a while.

I know Carrie is feeling OK 'cos she's already planning what we're doing when Danny and Sean get here tomorrow. I rang Sean today and he was ironing all of their clothes and packing their suitcase. Sean kept screaming and asking how hot it was and which clubs we were all going to. Danny was working today at Working Magic, he helped me get loads of jobs when I lived in London. Danny and Sean live together in London now. They've got a flat in Kilburn.

Kezia just asked me if Sean was still queer, so I says to Kez, 'Yeah, well he was last time I saw him, Kez, I reckon being gay is sort of an ongoing plan for Sean. Least, I hope so or Danny is going to be well narked.'

So then Kezia says that being gay don't have to be for ever 'cos her nan June used to go to a Jamaican church where they used to cure it by sticking their hands on your head and shouting at you and if that don't work the Pastor just makes your family lock you in the house.

So I says to Kez that I don't think Sean and Danny want to be 'cured'. I think they're proper happy. Well Kezia agreed with that and said there ain't nothing wrong with being a batty in her eyes anyway so I says, ' 'Ere, Kez, it's probably a good idea not to say batty to Sean and Danny 'cos that's not a nice word. It's a bit like them deciding to call you "wigga" and you hate that don't you?'

So Kezia just nods and thinks a bit and says, 'Oh OK, well what DO I call them? Fairies?' We all agreed that wasn't as bad. Sort of. Kezia ain't a bad person. She's just never ever been outside Goodmayes much. I used to say daft stuff like that once.

We're going to the beach today 'cos it's another SCORCHER and then we're going to a karaoke competion at the NightFever Bar in the West End. Carrie is determined to win the two-hundred-and-fifty euro prize and get spotted by a record producer. And all the Catford boys are coming too, and loads of other randoms from our apartments. THIS IS GOING TO BE WELL JOKES.

SUNDAY 13TH JUNE

7am – OH MY LIFE. I think I've just had the best night of my whole life EVER. I never want to leave Ibiza. Never. What have I got to go home for? I just want to stay here and have nights like this until the day I die. We've just all been out to NightFever to the karaoke. A whole big crowd of us went from the apartments La Paradiso. It was brilliant. We all headed down to the West End of San Antonio where there's loads of streets of bars and clubs and there's thousands and thousands of kids our age everywhere. And everyone seems either drunk or off their heads and everyone is out to have a good time.

Honestly, everywhere I looked I saw another crowd of bare choong single boys walking down the road looking all tanned and buff. It's like being in heaven. Kezia managed to pull this bare choong black lad from

Coventry called Benj before we'd even left the first bar! Kezia is terrible ain't she? I hope she's being careful.

So we all got to NightFever and it was jam-packed full, with a massive queue outside, so they were doing one-in one-out. It was six euros to get in and if you entered your name for karaoke you got a free drink with Absinthe and Sunny D in it called an 'Epileptic Fit'. So Carrie put her name down for about three tracks by Mariah Carey, then me and Uma put our names down to sing 'Breaking Free' from *High School Musical* 'cos that's one we used to sing together when we did the washing-up in London. Kez didn't put her name down for a song 'cos she'd disappeared off with Benj and we never saw her again. Well the night was hilarious. Taz got up and sang a Craig David song trying to do all the fast-rap bits which he totally couldn't, then Leon did an old fashioned song by Elton John and he was really good like he'd practised loads of times in his bedroom! Then me and Uma sang 'Breaking Free' which sounded bloody awful but we didn't care and everyone was booing us to sit down so we just sang even louder and tried to do harmonies HA HA HA LMAO!

Then Carrie did her songs and she was quite good really. I mean, even if she didn't reach the high notes she was trying for she kept on waving her arms around like a proper singer so she looked really professional. Carrie didn't win the prize 'cos this girl from Watford did, singing 'How Do I Live' by Leanne Rhymes and she sounded AMAZING. Like someone who'd be in the final three in *X-Factor*. She definitely didn't sound like someone 'killing a donkey with a hammer' which is what one of the glass collectors said about Carrie's singing. Carrie says she's not bothered 'cos the criticism she got was contructive and she's going to take it on board and give one hundred and ten per cent next week.

So, anyway, Taz was being a major flirt with me all night. Carrie was narked for about five minutes then she got off with a lad from Manchester. PHEW.

Anyway, Taz kept putting his hands around my waist and telling me how pretty I looked and how much I suited having a tan. Then he started saying how amazing it was that I lived in Goodmayes and he lived in Catford 'cos we could see each other when we got home. LIKE WE HAD A FUTURE TOGETHER! And OK this sounds a bit mad when I write it down but it was really sweet 'cos I could see he totally meant it. And before I knew it we were snogging like crazy right in front of everyone and he was lifting me off the ground! And Taz smelled so gorgeous and he's got amazing muscley arms. And for the whole of the rest of the night I was sitting on his knee and he was kissing me and then when we walked home back to the apartments and my feet were killing me 'cos of those TopShop high heels I borrowed off Carrie which had given me blisters, so Taz made me take the shoes off and he picked me up and gave me a fireman's lift home. He kept smacking my bum and I was screaming and laughing and it was the best feeling in the world, ever.

So when we got back Taz tried to convince me to come back to his apartment with him for another drink but I said no 'cos I knew it was full of all the other boys sitting up smoking so we'd not be alone. Plus I wanted to check if Kezia had showed up home too. So I came back to our apartment and now I'm lying in bed and there is no Kezia and no Carrie, just Uma, who is snoring and I feel properly mentally weird and I'm wondering how hard it is to get from Catford to Goodmayes? Does the train ticket cost much? Do the trains run proper regular? I hope so 'cos I want to go and see Taz loads and loads and loads 'cos I think that I'm falling in love.

MONDAY 14TH JUNE

4pm – By the pool. Sean and Danny are here! It is well good to see them.

OMG I forgot how buff Danny was until I opened the apartment door yesterday and there he was with his sunglasses on and a short-sleeved pale blue Armani shirt and some navy shorts and his really toned brown legs and white Reeboks, smelling of Hugo Boss aftershave.

'Man,' Kezia sighed, 'Dat is a proper waste of a boy.' Then she says, 'Oi, Shiz, are you SURE I can't put my hands on him and try to, y'know, cure him.' So I says to Kezia no, Danny would prefer it if we didn't touch, feel, kiss or nuzzle him in any way and BELIEVE ME I HAVE TRIED 'cos I made a right tit of myself last year trying to get off with him before I realised he was totally one hundred per cent not into girls. It was well shameful.

So then Sean ran in and gave us all massive hugs and he was being all mega-hyped up, just like he was when he was in our class at Mayflower. He was telling us about their HappyFlight Airlines flight which took them from Gatwick to Heathrow with an unscheduled stop in Donegal, Ireland, 'cos someone noticed smoke coming out of one of the wings. So the plane did an emergency landing and then the pilot got out and went up some stepladders and hit it with a hammer and then they set off again. That sounded pretty scary but we all agreed that if you're getting a fourteen quid return ticket to Ibiza, plus six tokens off the back of the Extra Hot Pepperami, well you can't really get the hump about a bit of danger can you? It keeps things exciting.

So we all had some vodka and Vimtos on our balcony and then we went down to one of the beach bars nearby for Happy Hour. Me and Danny were walking together behind everyone and he says to me, 'There's something different about you, Shiraz Bailey Wood. What is it? Did you get back with Wesley Barrington Bains II?'

So I says, 'No.' and then I told him all about Wesley and Sooz-who-needs-an-emergency-deep-conditioning-treatment-in-her-hair and how that was all over now for good. And then I told Danny about Taz, the fireman from

Catford. Well I couldn't stop rambling on and on 'cos I'm proper excited as Taz had texted me earlier asking to see me again that night and this time we were going out to get some Chinese food together. And to be honest I didn't think I'd be able to eat 'cos I just felt sick every time I thought about him. So I said all this to Danny and I says, 'Danny I really think I've found someone.' Well Danny smiled a bit and says in his funny *Coronation Street* accent, 'Oi, Shizzle, chill your boots darling. You've only known this guy a couple of days!' And I says, 'Yeah, but when you meet someone you just KNOW don't you?' and Danny thought for a bit and then he says, 'Yeah, you do. It's just that sometimes it turns out that you don't.'

I dunno what he meant by that.

Well, anyway, me and Taz went out for the Chinese food last night and we had such an amazing time and I was out all night with him drinking and dancing doing all sorts of stuff I don't want my mother to ever find out about and I keep checking my phone today 'cos I can't wait to see him again.

TUESDAY 15TH JUNE

From – dianewood500@wideblueyonder.com
To – theshizzlebizzle@hotmail.com

Hello Shiraz! This is your mum. Well there's a shock eh? Old mother ain't as daft as you all think is she?? HA HA HA. I am getting this interweb thingybob sussed. This is my first ever email. Our Cava-Sue is helping but I'm proper proud of myself!! Honest to God Shiraz, I cannot for the life of me understand how this letter gets down the phone line and finds you in Ibiza. Cava-Sue reckons it is to do with satellite thingies up near the moon beaming stuff down. She says I don't need to worry about that and just write something so I will.

Anyway hello love, I hope you are well and you are having a lovely holiday and the weather has kept nice for you and that you are being a good girl and not getting in any trouble. I know you can't ring us 'cos you haven't got that foreign call roaming thing on your phone have you? Good job too 'cos I keep seeing it on *Watchdog* and it's proper daylight robbery. We are OK in Thundersley Road I suppose. We had ourselves a bit of a drama on Saturday night with Murphy. He got brought home from Ilford Mall by the police after him and Tariq and that 'Sizzle' character he's running about with got in a fight with some other boys from the Lark Rise Estate. He's got a black eye now. He looks like a bleeding thug. I'm going up the wall with him Shiraz, honestly I am. The police brought him back indoors to me and said I should deal with him. So I says to the bloody policeman, What do you want me to do with him? He's six foot one and he weighs twelve stone? Shall I put him over my knee and smack his bum? Well the policeman said no please don't do that Mrs Wood 'cos we'd have to do you for common assault. Bloody wonderful eh?

Anyway lovely, aside from that we are all fine. Cava-Sue is having a right old adventure at work with those nutters on Bridge Avenue. Fin is sprouting teeth every day. The dogs are getting along good together aside from Penny and her non-stop bum sniffing. We ain't going to get burgled while we've got these two on guard though are we? Zeus is a big soft thing really though. Are you sure Uma wants Zeus back? He seems proper settled here. That is a hint by the way. HA HA HA.

Oh, and before I forget, I saw Wesley Barrington Bains II yesterday. He was just coming out of the pizza shop carrying a big pizza and a bottle of Coke and getting in his car. He had some blonde girl in the front seat, like they were having a night in together. He looked OK anyway. He beeped his horn at me. He's such a nice lad. Proper genuine he is. Oh my life look at all this Shiraz I've written a book ain't I! I'm going to send this now 'cos I need to let the dogs out for widdle and get myself to bed. Speak to you soon – your mum xx

Personalise your messages at wideblueyonder with smiles! Go to www.smileyfactory-wby.com and make your mails miles better!

WEDNESDAY 16TH JUNE

2pm – Here we all are at Las Cartinas Beach. It's this little sandy beach about four miles from San Antonio. Carrie made us get a bus out here 'cos she was dying to see what all the fuss is about 'cos they always go on about it on

1Xtra and *Kiss* and *MTV*. Plus that DJ bloke, Frankie, who Carrie met on the plane told us that Las Cartinas is where anyone worth knowing goes during the day. It's a bit mental here to be honest. The whole beach and the tiny bar are totally full of people who ain't been to bed since going clubbing from the night before. So it's broad daylight sunny and there's a full-on party going on and loads of girls and boys, some in swimwear but some in last night's clothes, all dancing and shouting and screaming and they're all a bit cross-eyed and they're acting like it's still two in the morning but it ain't it's the next day!

Frankie said to Carrie that the police keep trying to shut this place down but it just starts up again. I can sort of see why the police wouldn't like it. It feels out of control and grown-ups hate young people doing stuff they ain't in control of don't they? It's bare jokes just lying in the sun watching it all. Uma and Carrie have been up dancing for the last hour.

Me and Carrie bumped into Frankie and his mates yesterday when we were going to the supermercado for more beer and Honey Nut Loops. Frankie pulled up in this well expensive jeep with blackened windows. The other three guys in the jeep all looked quite hard really, they had shaved heads and one had a cut eye. So Carrie was giggling and flirting with Frankie asking what he'd been up to this week and Frankie said, 'Oh nothing and everything really.'

Frankie said they'd just been to the airport to pick up a friend and now they were going to a bar to give something to someone. To be honest, everything Frankie said was proper vague, like he was talking in some sort of code. I think he's a bit of a weirdo to be honest but Carrie thinks he is LUSH and totally sophisticated and amazing and could be 'the one' and I know better than to try and talk her out of it when she's found 'the one', 'cos it happens a lot.

Anyway, I shouldn't be too mean 'cos Frankie said to us he can get us all on the VIP guest list tonight for 2-Hot-2-Be-Serious at Arrival. This is like the best night on the entire island. The tickets are about ninety euros each. I've texted Taz and asked if he wants to come but he's not texted back. I didn't hear much from him yesterday either. That is proper weird.

4pm – Still no message from Taz. I called him and it rang a few times and then went to voicemail. Is he blanking me? OH GOD I hope not. I'm not telling any of the girls about it. This is well embarrassing. Maybe he's lost his phone? I mean, it was him saying he was bloody falling in love with me the other night. It was him doing all the running. I don't understand this at all. Right, I'm not thinking about it. It's doing my head in.

6pm – OMG. That Frankie geezer sorted us out VIP wristbands for Arrival! We just picked them up from a record shop in San Antonio. All the guys in the record shop knew exactly who Frankie and his mates were the moment Carrie mentioned him. They all laughed a bit when she said Frankie was a DJ. Oh no. He must be a really rubbish one. Anyway Danny and Sean can come too now. And there's a free bar in the VIP area, too, which is lucky 'cos I am well beginning to run out of money. We're going out tonight at about midnight. I might leave Taz another message and tell him which bars we're going to be in. Maybe he's not well and he's been in bed and didn't get the other ones.

11pm – We're all getting ready to go! To be honest, I really think Carrie should put a thong on with that mini-dress. Especially if she's going to do high-kicks. It just ain't right.

11.15pm – Kezia is actually spewing BEFORE we've even left the apartment. This is some sort of record.

11.45pm – Wow. Uma is wearing this black backless dress by Vivienne Westwood that one of her big winning customers at the Imperial Palace bought her as a pressie. She looks proper beautiful in it standing smoking her Embassy Red on the balcony. It's funny 'cos Uma hasn't had one snog all holiday. She's not interested, she says. Uma says she's only got room for one bloke in her life and he's got four legs and a docked tail and a spikey collar and he loves her and doesn't cause her any grief. Uma's missing Zeus a lot. She keeps looking at his photos on her phone and making me say how cute he looks which is an odd thing to say about a photo of a massive slobbering dog destroying an Igglepiggle toy.

11.55pm – Still no message from Taz. I'm going to stick a note under his door before we leave.

THURSDAY 17TH JUNE

5am – I honestly bloody can't believe this has happened.

5.30am – WHAT A BLOODY TOTAL BLOODY PIG THAT BOY IS. I hate him. I bloody hate him. HE IS A TOTAL BLOODY PIG.

1pm – I'm proper upset today but I'm not letting it show in my face. That's one thing I've learned from Uma over the years, even back in the day when we'd stand in Mr Bombleclot's office at Mayflower and he'd be shouting at us telling us how scummy we both were and how we'd never be nothing ever just like the rest of our family, just like the rest of our estate. Well he could get me in tears sometimes but not Uma he couldn't. Uma would just stand there and her face would stay rock hard like a mask. That's why Uma's good at playing poker. She don't let anything show in her face. Uma says when people know what you're feeling, well that's when you're vulnerable. So I'm wearing my sunglasses today and my face is saying, 'I'm not bothered, bruv, jog on, 'cos I don't give a flying crap.'

3pm – OK, I'm going to write down what happened. That might make me feel better. Basically, me, Uma, Carrie, Sean, Kez and Danny all went out last night down to the bars on the beach and we had some

80

vodka Redbulls and we were all chatting and having a good time. We were in Café Mambo and there were fire-eaters and jugglers outside on the sand and Ronnie Skyro from KissFM was playing a set on the terrace and it was a really warm night and everything would have felt just perfect if I weren't waiting for a text that never came. So at about 1am we got taxis down to Arrival and there was a MASSIVE queue of about a thousand people outside but we went straight to the front 'cos we were VIPs.

Well, when we got inside there was about two thousand people inside all going proper mad on the dancefloor. I've never seen anything like it before in my whole life. There was about five different dancefloors and naked dancers in bodypaint dancing in cages and laser beams shooting everywhere and people dressed as giraffes and zebras walking about on stilts and girls in Las Vegas showgirl costumes walking about giving out free shots of Tequila. We all headed for the VIP area and showed our wristbands and went into this big, dark room where there was another dancefloor and another huge bar and there was all sorts of people in there that we sort of recognised from the telly, like two of the blonde girls off *Hollyoaks* and a boy who was once on *Dream Team* on Sky One. Well Carrie went proper loopy when she saw him and started doing her subtle sexy dancing which involved waggling her bum in his face and jumping up and down with her scones bouncing about. I think he must have got the hint 'cos he knocked back his drink and left soon after that.

Anyway, we were all having a bare jokes time and I was trying not to think about Taz 'cos I knew it was daft to let that spoil getting VIP tickets and going clubbing with the girls but then the DJ played 'Soulsearcher' by ForeverUndone which was the song me and Taz both agreed was our favourite song right now and we'd been dancing to it the other night after we went for the Chinese together. This was the night he said he couldn't wait to introduce me to his mother in Catford 'cos she would love me. Well I started feeling sad then and Kezia must have noticed 'cos she says, 'Oi, Shiz, wa gwan? Wots with your face?' and I says, 'Oh nothing. I'm OK.' And Kez laughs and says, 'Oh my God, there are so many bare choong boy dem in here, innit? I don't know which one to choose!'

So I groans a bit and says, 'Oh, mate, I'm not in the mood tonight.'

And Kez says, 'Why not?'

So I says, 'Aw I sort of started seeing someone.'

And Kez goes, 'Who?!' and I says, 'Taz.'

Well Kez looks at me like I'm having a mentaloid fit or something and she says, 'Shiz, you ain't seeing Taz. Taz has got a girlfriend. A proper serious one. He lives with someone in Catford. He's got a kid too.'

Well honest to God, I felt like someone had smashed me in the stomach with a sledgehammer. But the thing was I knew Kez was quite off her head so I thought maybe she'd got it wrong, so I says, 'No he hasn't! Are you sure, Kez? But the Catford boys said they were all single!' And Kez laughs and said, 'Yeah that's what they said but they ain't clever, innit? I soon tripped Leon up on that one and he told me everything. They've all got girlfriends! Oh bloody hell, Shiz, I thought you knew this! I thought you weren't bothered.' So I says to Kezia, 'Of course I'm bloody bothered, Kezia! Why would I not be bothered?!' So Kez says, 'Well what's to be bothered about? You're on holiday! Nothing matters on holiday! No one knows that I've got a baby girl do they? They don't know Uma is a croupier and that's why she keeps winning their cash! Taz don't know you're still hung up on Wesley does he?!'

'I'm not hung up on Wesley!' I says.

'Oh OK, I got that one wrong then,' says Kezia. 'The point is, we've all been telling little fibs. We just didn't get caught. That's 'cos we're cleverer than them boys, innit?' Well my head was spinning now. Then Kez laughs and says, 'Like all that stuff Taz is chatting about being a fireman. He ain't a bloody fireman at all!'

'What?' I says, 'cos this was just about the bloody limit now. 'What do you mean he ain't a fireman?!'

And Kez says, 'Oh bloody hell, didn't you know that either? Taz wanted to be a fireman but he failed the exam 'cos of his eyes, so he works in a Wild Bean Café in a BP Connect garage instead.'

Well, my memory ain't that clear after that point 'cos

things started to go a bit blurry. I know I decided to have a shot of tequila and then another one and then some other stuff that was going about and all I remember is that when we eventually got back to the apartments the Catford boys, including Taz, were out smoking on their balcony and there was a whole other load of girls we've never seen before out there partying with them.

But I'm not going to cry about it or anything 'cos as I say, I'm not going to let it show on my face.

9pm – I've just been down to Café Del Mar, this little beach bar in San Antonio near our apartments. I have just watched my first ever Ibizan sunset. We've managed to bloody miss it every single night of the holiday so far. Don't ask me how. Time just sort of flies past in Ibiza.

We got down Café Del Mar at about five and grabbed a little table together outside, just us four girls. Then we ordered some beers and sat and chilled out for a bit watching as the sun began to sink down into the sea. It was well beautiful. And yes it did make me think about my life and where it was heading and all that sort of stuff 'cos before I knew it massive drops of water were coming down my cheeks behind my sunglasses and I couldn't stop crying.

Well Uma was first to notice. 'Shiraz!' she says, 'What's the matter?!'

So I says, 'Oh nothing. It's nothing.'

And then Kezia says, 'Oh God, Shiz, is that about that

clown Taz or whatever he's calling himself? He ain't worth crying about. What a rotter he is! You're better off without him.' And then Kezia told Carrie and Uma what had happened and everyone was proper outraged at what a knob Taz was. I love my friends, they are properly amazing.

Then Carrie gave me a big hug and told me everything was going to be fine, and she started scheming about breaking into the Catford boys' apartment when they were out and cutting holes in all of Taz's jeans and underpants. I said nice idea but that wouldn't help anything.

Then Uma offered to go and have a 'quiet word' with Taz and tell him she knew which bloody BP Connect he ran the coffee machine in and she'd be informing her brother Clinton to drop by when he got out of Chelmsford Jail. And Kezia said she was going to tell every girl she met for the rest of the holiday that Taz had a willie so little that he had to get it out his undies with tweezers when he went for a wee. Well that was the first time I laughed all day.

I don't know what I'd do without these girls. Honest to God. I'd go mad. So we sat for ages then and we watched the sunset and that chilled me out a bit and we were talking about boys and how much hassle they cause us girls. Uma was saying she can't be bothered getting involved with boys END OF 'cos she thinks they're all liars. Uma says every one of her mother Rose's boyfriends was the same in the end. Off out tapping off with other women. And her dad was the same. And her brothers are like that too. Can't keep anything good going. Always bloody lying. Uma says you never find a boy who just is who he is. Well aside, Uma says, from my ex-bloke Wesley who was a proper gent, 'cos he was always straight down the line, but aside from that they're all a bunch of wastemen. You're better off with a dog, says Uma.

Then Kez says that she didn't really agree with Uma one hundred per cent 'cos she can't stop loving boys even though she knows they're all players. Kez says she can't stop chasing them 'cos she loves that bit at the beginning when boys are all buzzing to see you and telling you you're gorgeous and saying they love you 'cos basically they want to get you into bed. Kez says she always sort of hopes that they'll carry on being like that afterwards which they never do, but that don't stop her having fun in the meantime. Kez says she always hopes someone will love her properly one day like Luther used to love her before he dumped her or like Wesley Barrington Bains II loved me before we went our different ways. But Kez says that never seems to happen and to be honest now she feels like it never will now she's got Tiq. Kez says she don't think boys really want her 'cos she's got major baggage. That was proper sad when Kez said that.

Carrie said that she finds it proper easy to meet boys that she fancies 'cos she fancies all sorts of boys. Quiet ones, noisy ones, black ones, white ones, Bengali ones,

Vietnamese ones, rich ones, not that rich ones, whatever. She just likes boys.

But the thing is she never stays interested in them. Carrie says boys always start to get on her nerves eventually. Carrie says for example, when she was with Saf and she'd be knocking about with me and Wesley, she used to sit there in the back seat of Wes's banana-yellow Golf when we were driving somewhere and she'd listen to me and Wes chatting on and on and on together and we always had a good laugh with each other and she used to think to herself, 'God why aren't me and Saf like that? Why don't we always have a good laugh?'

I felt a bit sick when I heard them talking about Wes. I started thinking about him and Sooz going for their night in with their big pizza. I used to love me and Wes's nights in together when I was knackered after working at Mr Yolk and he'd pick me up in his Golf and we'd go and get a Hawaiian Extra Hot pizza and the bloke in the pizza shop knew us so he'd just put Wes's jalapeños on one side and the pineapple on the other 'cos I can't eat jalapeños and Wes don't do 'savoury with fruit'. Then we'd pay for a Sky Box Office movie and lie on the couch and if it was one of them exploding car movies Wes always bloody wants to watch I'd end up falling asleep halfway though. I miss that.

Anyway me and the girls chatted on about boys for ages and by this point the sun had totally vanished and it was dark so we decided to go back to the apartments and get showered and glammed up to go out for some food. And I've been feeling really weird and confused ever since then 'cos I've realised that I don't care about Taz any more. Not one little bit. I seriously don't care at all. He means nothing to me. He never did if I think straight. What I'm freaked out about is something I've just worked out while I was watching the sunset. Something I need to sort out as soon as possible. 'Cos, yeah, I know that most boys tell lies and ain't worth nothing at all, but there's one boy out there who is solid gold and always keeps it real. And I've bloody gone and let him slip through my fingers.

FRIDAY 18TH JUNE

From – theshizzlebizzle@hotmail.com
To – thegoodmayesdetonator@hotmail.com

Hello Wes, it's Shiraz here. How are you? I'm OK. Ibiza is good fun. We've been having a good time. You know what Kezia and Carrie are like?! It ain't been dull. I've got a good tan too. I think you'd like Ibiza, Wes, 'cos there are loads of bars like ones you like with Premier League showing and places where you can get full English breakfast all day long even at midnight.

Look, Wes, can I be proper honest with you for a second? I don't want to drop all this crap on you and spoil your day or nothing but I need to say this and get it off my chest.

I think I might have made a mistake with all this me and you splitting up stuff. I know I've got a proper cheek saying this and I don't have no right to stir this all up again but it's taken me to come to Ibiza and have some space to see that me and you are meant to be together. Wes I know I have proper messed this all up and I'm a pain in the arse but I am well sorry.

I miss you, Wes. I ain't never been happy about you being with Sooz and the thought of you two indoors together having a pizza is killing me. Deep down do you still feel a bit the same about me like you did? That time we snogged back in April when you came to see me in London, that weren't just a snog was it? I think it meant something more. I think it meant that after all this time we are still properly in love. Oh, bloody hell, Wes, I am sorry for this email. I hope you ain't annoyed at me for saying this. Please write back and tell me what you think.

Love – Shiraz Bailey Wood xxx

SATURDAY 19TH JUNE

Midnight – It's only midnight on a Saturday night but I'm lying in bed 'cos I am absolutely knackered. I think my body has given up now. It's finally had enough. It needs a night off. We've been out every single night for ELEVEN NIGHTS! My feet are sore and covered in blisters from dancing in high heels. My shoulders have been burned red, gone dark brown and are now covered in minging flaky skin. My hair is dry and frazzled from lying in the sun and never getting enough time in the shower to condition it properly. I've got no clean clothes left either. Plus I'm almost skint. I'm down to my last twenty-five euros. I'm hoping Uma will give me a loan for the last few days.

And as for the apartment, well it looks like Al Qaeda has been round and left a bomb. Bless Uma, she tried her best but even she's given up now.

Uma says if Kezia is determined to live like a bloody pig in a sty spreading her crap wherever she wants it then that's Kezia's perogative. Uma says from now on she's only washing up her own plates and that the cups under Carrie and Kezia's bed, the ones with mould in them, they're not her concern. Kezia says she ain't bothered what Uma does and doesn't wash. Kezia says why's Uma so stressed anyway if there's a trail of ants coming in from the balcony and eating our Honey Nut Loops, 'cos they're only ants aren't they? Ants never killed anyone! Carrie has been trying to clean the place up a bit to keep the peace, but seeing as Mrs Raziq does everything for her at Draperville, Carrie ain't exactly practical around the house. She makes things worse, not better. I can't believe no one has slapped anyone else yet 'cos aside from all the mess and the ants none of us have had much sleep. It can get a bit tense, then we all have a drink and we forget about it again.

Anyway, we've just been down at NightFever again

tonight for the karaoke competition. It was Carrie who was demanding to go, OF COURSE. Carrie still don't seem to have achieved any closure about that girl last week, 'stealing her prize'. I wasn't much in the mood for karaoke to be honest. I wanted to go back down to the internet café and check if my Wes had replied. He hadn't written back when I checked this morning at nine and at lunchtime or at six this evening. I checked my sent box to see if it had gone and it was definitely in there too. I'll check again in the morning.

When I told Carrie earlier on that I was thinking about not coming out Carrie says I've GOTTA come out tonight 'cos we're getting picked up by Frankie in his Jeep. Carrie said me and Uma had to glam ourselves up 'cos we were meeting Frankie's mates and we were going to have the most amazing night of the holiday so far. Kezia was invited too but she already had a date with this boy called Tabbo she'd met that day at the tattoo parlour. Kezia had the rest of the dolphin on her shoulder coloured in today and IBIZA written under it in red ink as a tribute to this holiday. It's gone a bit crusty already but Kezia is sure it's going to look MINT once all the scabs fall off. Kezia says she don't care if she's a bit scabby tonight 'cos Tabbo has got a scabby arm too. Tabbo's just had his hero Vin Diesel tattoed on his forearm. When we met Tabbo today Uma saw it and goes, 'Is that Homer Simpson?' Tabbo didn't speak to us much after that. OH MY DAYZ that was funny.

So, anyhow, Frankie turns up at the Apartments La Paradiso tonight at about eight and he pulls up in his Jeep playing some old-skool Biggy Smalls track with the windows wound down. Taz and Leon and them lot were on their balcony watching and they looked well gobsmacked which was a good thing I suppose. And as the Jeep pulled up all I could smell was aftershave and skunk 'cos someone inside was obviously smoking a big blunt. Me, Uma and Carrie climbed into the back seat, Frankie was driving and in the passenger seat was his mate Marcellus, this buff black boy who looked a bit like something off a Channel U video.

Frankie said we all look beautiful tonight like supermodels or something and Carrie giggled and flapped her eyelashes at him and I said, 'Thanks.' But Uma didn't say anything at all. Uma just looked at Frankie's Rolex and at the mini TV screens in the back of the seats and nudged my arm and rolled her eyes a bit.

So we got down to NightFever and for some reason this time we didn't have to queue or pay at the door 'cos Frankie and Marcellus knew the bouncers. Then Carrie was going to put her name down to sing some songs but Frankie says she didn't need to bother she should just tell him what she wanted to sing and she could sing whenever she wanted. So she said she wanted to sing 'We Belong Together' by Mariah Carey and then Marcellus went and had a word with the DJ and before we knew it, it was Carrie's go next, which was weird 'cos there was loads of people who'd got there before us. The whole night was a bit like that really. 'Cos there were no seats, but suddenly we got a booth to sit in with a table and waitress service and a bottle of champagne. The manager kept on coming over and talking to Frankie and Marcellus about 'business' that didn't sound anything like DJing and sending us drinks on the house. The funniest thing was when it came to announce the winner of the karaoke contest, 'cos Carrie had won. She won two hundred and fifty euros! Now this was totally unbelievable 'cos NO WAY was Carrie Draper the best singer, and I'm sorry 'cos I know she's my bezzie and everything, but one girl from Newcastle had nearly everyone almost in tears when she sang that Westlife song 'Flying Without Wings'. Carrie wasn't sounding that great tonight at all. In fact when Carrie was doing her Mariah song, Uma whispered to me that she didn't mean to be nasty or nothing but Carrie was a bit rubbish, and I whispered back to Uma yeah, to be honest it reminded me of the sound my nan made when I took her up to Whipps Cross Hospital to have her ingrown toenail cut out without any anaesthetic.

Me and Uma came home after that 'cos we fancied getting a kebab and an early night. Carrie stayed out with Frankie. When we left she was sitting on his knee with her arms around his shoulders counting her two hundred and fifty euros with a face on like she'd just won the lottery.

SUNDAY 20TH JUNE

12pm – OMG. Still no reply from Wesley. Wesley always taps me back. Even if he don't really have nothing to say. That's what Wesley does. He always makes time for me, 'cos I'm his friend. Why hasn't he replied? I bet it's that BITCH Sooz stopping him checking his emails. I bet she's got all sorts of BORING things she'd rather they do instead like go to B&Q and look at the display of houseplants or go to a car boot sale or drive her down to Marks and Spencer's so she can buy more acrylic trousers and jackets that make her look like a bloody thirty-five-year-old weather girl off TV. Or maybe they're having another pizza. Well I hope she's enjoying their bloody pizza. I hope they get an Extra Hot and she suddenly realises she's allergic to spicy beef and her head swells up all massive like a hot air balloon with yellow patches of pus all over it. I hope that happens. Honest to God I do. No actually I DON'T. I don't care at all what happens to either of them. I should never have sent that stupid email. I'm sick of coming down this stupid internet café. The two Ibizan girls who own it keep giving me sad looks every time I come in like they know this is a boy problem. This morning they even gave me a FREE CREDIT and a cup of coffee out of pity.

7pm – Still no reply from Wesley! I've just been lying on the beach sunbathing with Carrie, and I told her that I mailed him and she says, 'Why?!' and I says, ''Cos I think I might have maybe made a mistake?'

So Carrie sat there all stunned for a bit and didn't say anything and then she says, 'So what's he saying to that then?'

So I told her he'd never mailed me back yet. And she says, 'Since when?' and I says, 'Since Friday.'

Well Carrie didn't look too hopeful when I said that. Then she said that maybe if that's not meant to be, then what I should be thinking about is the future. Carrie says that's why I've got to come out with her on a double date tonight with Frankie and his mate Big Terry and go for dinner at a posh restaurant on the other side of the island. Carrie says I will love Big Terry as he is sweet.

At first I said, 'No way.' But then I thought, 'She's right, I should be thinking about the future! Not waiting for an email that ain't ever coming!' So I says to Carrie, 'What's Big Terry like?' Carrie says, 'Oh well, he's called Terry and he's really big.' So I says, 'Well, Cazza, I got no money I'm down to my last fifteen euros,' and Carrie says don't worry about money 'cos the boys have got plenty of it. So I says to Carrie how do they make so much money DJing 'cos they never ever seem to play and she says, 'Oh, Big Terry isn't a DJ he owns a security company supplying doormen to clubs in Ibiza. You'll love him!' Then she says, ''Ere, Shiz, why don't you put on my black Morgan strappy dress and those pink Jimmy Choo heels that my mum lent me and your big hoops. Do the whole Shizglam thing! Go on! We're going out partying with some of the most fun people on the island! This is real Ibiza! Not just staggering about the West End with all the tourists!' Uma was keeping her eyes shut on her sun lounger pretending to be asleep right through this chat. She knew she was next in line to get lumbered with Big Terry.

I'm going to go out tonight. I'll just pop down and check my mail once more before I get ready.

1am – OH MY LIFE. OH MY BLOODY LIFE.

Baby Jesus in heaven above, what did I do to deserve Carrie Draper as a friend? Why, oh why, oh WHY do I ever let her fix me up on double dates? Why? And what goes through her teeny-tiny little pink sparkly brain when she finds me someone? I don't understand!! So Frankie and Big Terry arrive tonight to pick us up. Big Terry was in the passenger seat of Frankie's Jeep when they pulled up but he got out so Carrie could sit in the front. Well when he got out of the Jeep I felt like turning round on the heels of Carrie's mum's silly 'cost about £400 make you walk like an Emu shoes' and legging it down the street.

BIG TERRY WAS ENORMOUS. He was about two metres tall and he must have weighed about 150 tonnes. And one very important fact Carrie neglected to tell me was that he had a bloody beard and a moustache. HE LOOKED LIKE A BEAR.

'You have got to be bleeding kidding me!' I said to Carrie under my breath when I saw him. Big Terry was wearing a black shirt and black trousers and black tie with red-and-white playing cards on it! He looked sort of embarrassed. NO BLOODY WONDER WITH THAT FACIAL FOREST. So I got in the Jeep and we both stared at each other and didn't say much and then Frankie said he was driving us to an amazing restaurant that served great seafood. Well all I could see in my head then was Big Terry on all fours in a mountain stream catching live salmon in his gob like a grizzly bear I once saw on Terrifying Beasts Weekend on the Discovery Channel.

So, we went to this restaurant in a place called Es Cana and Frankie was talking a lot about how much money he has and how he has a big house in Kent and how he knows everybody worth knowing in Ibiza and basically about how amazing he is full stop – only stopping now and again for Carrie and Big Terry to agree with Frankie about how amazing he is too. Then Frankie ordered some champagne and he pointed at this big sad-looking lobster what was sitting in a bucket of ice and said, 'That one.'

Then a bloke in an apron grabbed the poor thing and smacked it about a bit and boiled it and stuck it on our table with a hammer and a load of what looked like medieval torture tools you might see in the London Dungeons. Then Frankie started bashing the dead lobster to bits and feeding Carrie bits and knocking back champagne and ordering more and to be honest I didn't feel hungry by this point.

Well not for lobster. I could have deffo eaten a nice plain Hawaiian Hot with the jalapeños just on one side, sharing it with a bloke who didn't look like he was trapped inside a bloody bear football mascot costume.

Well, after dinner, which Frankie paid for without even blinking at the massive five hundred euro bill, the boys wanted us all to go to a party at a villa on the other side of San Antonio where there was going to be loads of club promoters and models and champagne and all sorts of other stuff.

I didn't want to go at all 'cos I could tell Big Terry had the hots for me and he had big sweat patches in the armpits of his shirt and lobster in his beard and down his playing-card tie and I was starting to get sick explosions in my mouth just looking at him. So I says to Carrie I'd rather go home thank you and she says, 'What are you mental or something?' so I says, 'No, I want to go back to the apartment.' So Carrie says well fine but she's going to go to the party and I tried to tell her not to but she said, 'Oh stop being an old woman, Shizza.'

So they dropped me off at the apartment block and I came indoors and I've been thinking about it all and about Wesley and about why I can't just let myself go with the flow like Carrie Draper does and thinking that maybe I am acting like a bloody old woman? And Carrie's just sent me a text from the party saying it is the most glamorous thing she has ever been to and everyone is totally off their heads and all the girls here look like WAGs and I'm totally mugging myself off not being here. So I've just taken my make-up off and counted the twenty-five euros I got left in my pocket and got into bed and Uma and Kez are off out somewhere and I want to go to sleep but I can't 'cos I feel proper confused and alone.

MONDAY 21ST JUNE

From – thegoodmayesdetonator@hotmail.com
To – theshizzlebizzle@hotmail.com

Aight Shiz, its well gud to hear from u innit. I been thinkin every day about u and how u iz getting on with all those mentalists in Ibiza. Hope u'z been avvin a gud time. Fings are OK here with me, innit. Bin proper busy at work and with uvver stuff innit. Look Shiz, this msg wot u have sent has put me in a bad position with Sooz right coz I have had to lie and say I never got it and you know I don't like to lie to people innit. The fing is, Shiraz, I think that maybe we should both just forget what u sed in that last message coz it just makes things proper messy and I want us to try and stay friends coz u iz important to me even if we aint boyfriend-girlfriend no more and I am with Sooz. Sorry, Shiz, but I wanted you to hear this from me not no one else but Sooz moved into my flat this weekend, innit. That's just the way it is, Shiz. I dunno what to say, innit. You know I'm not gud with this sort of shit innit. Look I gotta go now. Take care of yourself. Wesley x

2pm – Carrie's just got back from that villa party she was at with Frankie and found me on the balcony reading Wesley's email for the two hundreth bloody time. The girls at the internet café let me print it out and take it home for free. To be honest I think they just wanted me to leave the café 'cos I was sitting in the window bawling with my face all covered in snot which wasn't doing much for their profits. Carrie's just read the email about four times trying to work out if it's as 'jog on Shiraz don't ever ring me again THE END' as it sounds to me.

'OK,' Carrie said. 'So he says he's thought about you every day and he's wondering how you're getting on but he's asked that bird of his to move in with him. And he wants you to be mates but you can't mail him 'cos he can't tell her when you do and at the end he's all "take care of yourself" and ONE KISS? One bloody measly kiss? He's having a laugh with that, ain't he?' 'I know!' I said to Carrie, 'I bloody know. What's that meant to mean? What is he trying to say?' I said.

So Carrie scrunched up her face and said, 'Well I think, Shiz . . . And I know you don't want to hear this . . . He's saying that it's over. He's moved in with someone. Who do we know that's moved in with anyone? Hardly anyone! That's what you do when you're thinking long term with someone, don't you? That's what you do when

100

you're sure what you're doing. That's why you never moved in with him, ain't it? I mean how many times did he ask you? You always said no.' Well I really started crying then, thinking about Sooz sitting in Wesley's flat overlooking Tilak's Pakora factory, eating my Extra Hot pizza and falling asleep in MY space on the sofa.

Well Carrie let me cry for ages and she gave me a cuddle and then she said, 'Well, you know something I think this is a good thing.'

So I says, 'HOW?'

''Cos today you're at rock bottom. But this email is closure, ain't it? And from today the only way is up. New life, new Shiz, new destiny!' said Carrie.

'Suppose so,' I says. 'It's time to do something new and adventurous, Shizzle. You can't keep on thinking of the past. It's the future what's important. Ain't it?' Carrie said.

'Yeah I know,' I says to her. So then Carrie looks at me with a naughty expression and she says, 'Good. I'm glad you said that. So I'm hoping you're going to join me on my next adventure then? Sounds like you might be up for it.'

'Why, what are you doing?' I said, knowing as ever it would be something mental.

'I'm not going home tomorrow, Shiraz,' she says, 'I'm not going back to Goodmayes. I'm staying in Ibiza. I'm getting a job and I'm staying in Ibiza for the rest of the summer, or maybe for ever. And I think you should too.'

From – theshizzlebizzle@hotmail.com
To – murphdog92@wideblueyonder.com

Allo Murphdog, it's Shizzle here. Murph I am really really extra sorry I ain't tapped you back sooner. Those emails u sent came thru as spam and I just found them in my junk folder tonight which is a right pain. If I had seen them sooner I would have written or called you bruv coz you sound proper sad. Murph I am worried about you. Mum said you've been fighting in the mall and getting black eyes? Murphy, you ain't a muppet I don't need to tell you that going round thinking you're a gangster in Ilford ain't a good idea. You're going to get merked. You know that. Why don't you drop all this gangsta shit and work out what it is you're really angry about coz it certainly ain't about some clowns from the Lark Rise having the nerve to come and buy a Twix on Thundersley Road London is it? This is all about you and Ritu and the fact that she's gone and left you and gone back to Osaka which weren't even a diss from her or nothing coz she had to go back to her studies. You need to sort that out and either find a way to make you and her work or move on and stop letting it spoil your life.

And Murph, if you do want to make it work then you should bloody make it clear to Ritu what you want from her and don't piss about for about three years coz, TAKE IT FROM ME Murph, I did this with my Wes and I made a right old arse-up of that one. You are the master of your own destiny, Murph. One of my old teachers said that me at school and it was the only bloody thing I learned that was useful.

Look Murph, I'm sorry for stressing you out and having a go at you but I'm only saying this coz you're my little brother and I love you to bits and at the end of the day I would do anything for you END OF. And I know you ain't ever going to say that back to me coz you're a big tough bloke and all that but I know you think that too so you don't need to. And with that in mind I was wondering if you'd tell Mother for me that I won't be flying back home tomorrow to Heathrow like I said I would coz I am staying in Ibiza with Carrie and getting a job as a dancer in a cage at a nightclub called Arrival.

Thanks for that Murph. Keep it real, blud. Your big sister, Shiraz xxxxxx

TUESDAY 22ND JUNE

12pm – Café Del Mar, San Antonio.

Uma has really really got the hump about me and Carrie not going home to Essex with her and Kezia today. Uma started off the morning properly going off her head shouting saying all sorts of rude words that I don't think I'll write in this diary in case our Fin ever picks it up by accident and becomes the most foul-mouthed child in Goodmayes.

So I says to Uma she should bloody chill out and I regretted that right away 'cos only a total mentalist would tell Uma Brunton-Fletcher to 'chill out'. Once Uma gets into full flow non-chilledness she ain't chilling out for nobody, and you can ask our old school caretaker at Mayflower Mr Hargrove about that, 'cos when we were in Year 7 he once watched her destroy his entire greenhouse with a hammer when they came to remove her from school to take her to the pupil referral unit. And, yeah, OK, Uma was a lot calmer than that today 'cos she didn't smash anything or punch anyone but her eyes were all wide and mental like she might, so I got all the blunt throwable objects like ashtrays and mugs out of the way before I sat down with her for our one-to-one chat.

'Shiraz,' Uma says to me lighting up an Embassy Red off another Embassy Red and blowing two thick blasts of smoke down her nostrils, 'Look, don't be an arse. I know we've had a good time here but the holiday is over. Just get on the bloody coach, come to the airport and come home.'

'No, Uma!' I said. 'I've got nothing to come home for. No job, no Wesley, no bloody bed even!'

'Exactly,' says Uma. 'That's why you need to go home, then. You need to sort that out and make some plans. Remember when I turned up at your flat in East London last year? I had nothing to bloody live for! No job, nowhere to live, no cash, my mother's house in Goodmayes had just been bust by the police again! But that's how life is, Shiz, you hit rock bottom and you build it all up again, don't you?' 'But why can't I do that in Ibiza? What's wrong with Ibiza?!' I went on to Uma. Then I had a mad thought and I said, 'Look! Why don't you stay too? There's casinos here in San Antonio. You could get a job here!' But Uma just shook her head and said, 'Shiraz, Mr Deng is moving me to a job next week where I can train to be a manageress. He's even got me a flat to live where I can take my Zeus. I ain't messing that up for anything. I've worked my arse off every day since last December to prove to him I'm not another knobhead who's going to let him down.'

Well I couldn't say nothing to that 'cos it was true.

'And anyways,' says Uma, a bit more quietly, 'I've got a prison visiting order to see Clinton in Chelmsford next Monday so I got that to look forward to as well.' Uma rolled her eyes when she said that and then she grabbed my hand and squeezed it and said, 'Look, Shiz. Please come home. You and Carrie can't be staying on here just 'cos that Frankie geezer is filling Carrie's head full of spit about how much he likes her. I wouldn't make any plans around Frankie. He's no good.'

So I had to laugh then, and I said, 'Oh Frankie's all right! He put in a word for us at Arrival. He got us jobs!'

Uma just shook her head at me and said, 'Don't be owing any favours to men like Frankie, Shiz. It ain't worth it. I've spent my whole bloody life surrounded by dodgy blokes like him with no jobs – or no jobs you can put your finger on what they do anyway – who still somehow have money and flash cars. It ain't nothing you want to be close to.' Well, I'm not being funny, but Frankie and Marcellus and Big Terry are nothing like the Brunton-

Fletchers. I don't think so anyhow. No offence to Uma but she is just proper anti-men full stop. She doesn't trust any of them and I can't say I blame her 'cos the men in her family are pigs. But I didn't have time to tell Uma that 'cos at this point Billy Big Gob the Happy Holiday Rep arrived banging on the door being really really bloody noisy telling us we had ten minutes to get out of our apartments 'cos the coach was here to pick us up for the airport.

So Uma and Kezia got on to the coach. Kezia was laughing her head off going, 'Shiz, you're nuts, bruv. I can believe Carrie doing this but man this is too jokes. Your mother is going to totally flip out!' Then she gave me and Caz a hug and got inside and sat on the back seat.

Then all the Catford boys came out with their suitcases, including Taz, which was a bit awkward for him I could tell 'cos he was all putting his head down and trying not to see me when I was standing there two metres away from him. He didn't say anything to me though. Probably 'cos I was doing my very best L'il Kim face like I might smack him one. He just scurried off on the coach like the little lying mouse he is. Then Wilf and Mavis came out and they'd clearly heard off Billy Big Gob that me and Carrie weren't coming home 'cos Mavis gave me twenty euros and told me and Carrie to buy a phonecard and tell our families where we were 'cos they'd be worrying about us. This made me feel quite bad 'cos I didn't want to tell Mavis that Carrie's got roaming on her phone so we could ring home any time. We just weren't phoning home 'cos we know they'll all go ballistic.

Then the coach doors shut and it set off and just as it was leaving Uma turned round and stared at me and Carrie, stood outside Apartments La Paradiso with our suitcases by our feet. She didn't say anything else. She just stared at us for a bit and didn't let anything show on her face then she put on her sunglasses and looked away and the coach disappeared.

We're in Café Del Mar now. Carrie is off somewhere talking on her phone to Rodriguez, Frankie's mate who is sorting us out with a room to live in while we work at Arrival. We're moving there tonight. It's going to be amazing.

SUNDAY 27TH JUNE

2pm – Villa Los Antilles – San Antonio.

It's four days since I've written anything in this diary. I just haven't had any time at all since we moved here. And I don't get too much privacy either 'cos this villa is proper jam-packed. There's got to be about thirty girls living here, five to a bedroom! I actually can't keep track of them all 'cos everyone sort of looks the same and everyone has friends staying over all the time. It's proper hectic, no one seems to ever go to bed and they're all from different parts of the world so every time you try to curl up on your camp bed and go to sleep all you can hear is people shouting on their mobiles in Spanish or Italian or Swedish.

All the girls in the villa came to Ibiza this year at some point on holiday and had such a good time they never went home and now they're working at Arrival as dancers. Well it's called dancing but it isn't really dancing as I've ever done it before, 'cos if I danced like this down at Jumping Jaks in Romford then a load of medics in white coats would arrive and sit on me then put me in a padded cell. Basically, what happens is, a minibus arrives here at the villa every night at 10pm and picks us all up and takes us to the club and then we all go into a big changing room at the back and take all our clothes off 'cos we need to put our bodypaint on. This is proper embarrassing to be honest 'cos the girls from Sweden and Italy don't give a damn who sees them in the buff and they walk about with their front bums out and everything and even try to talk to you with it twenty centimetres from your face. Noooooooo!

So me and Carrie always go in the corner so no one can see us and I choose dark green or navy blue paint and paint every bit of me from head to foot and then stick as many sequins and feathers over my bits as possible, then put some sort of pants over the whole lot too. Some of the other dancers are proper skinny size 4 or something and they paint themselves silver and don't wear bikini tops, just thongs, and they look proper amazing, although I know for sure now how they stay at size 0 and it ain't down to a healthy diet at all. It's down to all sorts of other stuff they're putting in their mouths and up their noses that I'm trying not to get involved with and I am trying my best to keep Carrie not involved too.

Anyway, at about 1am we all have to go and take our positions in different cages round the club and me and Carrie always get cages next to each other and then basically once the main room's DJ gets going we just have to dance. And keep on dancing all night long until 6am which is really quite a long time. The first night we did it on Tuesday I was totally embarrassed 'cos I thought everyone in the club would be staring at me and laughing, but then you start to realise that no one in the club really notices you're there at all.

And if somebody was to look at the dancers then they'd be staring at Kitty from Holland who can actually dance like something off a Justin Timberlake video and she's about a size 6 with big boobs and she covers herself in silver dust glitter and she can put her leg behind her ear and spin round on one foot. You'd certainly not be looking at Shiraz Bailey Wood, covered in bottle-green paint with big pants on over the top, basically doing star jumps and really bad 'pop 'n' lock' breakdance moves and sitting down every ten minutes for a rest 'cos she's totally out of breath and nearly needing an asthma inhaler.

It was sad last night 'cos Sean and Danny came up to

me in my cage at about 5am and said they needed to say goodbye 'cos they were flying home tomorrow. They were only out here for a week, it's passed so quickly. Danny gave me a hug, although not too tightly 'cos he didn't want to get green paint down his Paul Smith shirt. Danny looked a bit worried, and he said, 'Shiraz darling, do you think you're doing the right thing here?'

And I said, 'Yeah, course I am Danny! This is amazing! Why?'

'I don't know, babe,' says Danny. 'It's just y'know after that thing with that idiot Taz, and then you decide that you want to be back with Wes, and then Wes says there's no getting back together, then next thing you're living in Ibiza and dancing almost naked in a cage. It's a bit random isn't it, Shiraz?'

So I says to Danny, 'Oh don't worry about me, Danny, I'm always a bit random, innit? Anyway, I'm having the time of my life. I get paid to come to a nightclub!'

Danny did laugh when I said that and he said, 'Look, Shiraz Bailey Wood, please take care. Stay in touch, right? I'll be thinking about you.' Then he gave me all his spare euro notes 'cos he knew I'm totally skint and haven't had much to eat for days then they gave me a kiss and off they went. I don't know what Danny's so worried about. Of course I'm doing the right thing. I don't have no regrets. There's no point in regretting anything. You have to keep moving forward. Keep on keeping it real.

MONDAY 28TH JUNE

10pm – San Antonio – Hostal Anibal – Room 337.

Oh my dayz. Carrie and me are no longer working at Arrival. That means we no longer get free accommodation at the villa, which is a bit of a relief to be honest 'cos it was totally minging with all those girls in the same place and my bed was beside this well filthy girl called Annik from Belgium who never ever washed off her body paint. She just put more on over the sweat, and she took Es and cocaine all day and night long and at one point she left a used tampon floating in a cup beside her bed 'cos she couldn't be bothered to go to the loo. And if that ain't the most DIRTY VILE thing I have ever seen in my entire life and ever will see, then LORD GOD ABOVE, WHAT WILL BE?

So anyway, we ain't working as dancers any more for a few reasons, the main one being 'cos we were the crappest dancers in the world ever. And I've got to say here that Carrie was crapper than me 'cos by about 5am most mornings she was just whirling round and round on the spot with her arms out looking a bit like one of those twirling clothes drying things that mums put in their garden.

Myself, I'd sort of given up trying to do real dancing but I was still being enthusiastic doing a lot of pointing and clapping and the occasional 'reach for the lasers' move. But last night Rodriguez said that I wasn't putting enough energy into it and then Rodriguez asked me not to wear my green paint and pants costume 'cos some Scottish people were remarking that I looked like the Loch Ness Monster at a rave. Bloody cheek?

Then Rodriguez said that the look they were going for at Arrival was 'sexy alien from the planet Love,' then he pointed at Annik from Belgium and said that's what I should try to look like. So I says to Rodriquez that I had no intention of being like Annik from Belgium in any way 'cos she's got body odour that can choke you from a mile off and she's a phantom tampon-chucker. In fact just that morning I'd found another one in my shoe. Well Rodriguez got all arsey then and he told me I was one of the most troublesome dancers he had working for him and I shouldn't come back tomorrow night 'cos I was fired!

I was going to start kicking off at him then, but Carrie came up to me in tears and said she'd just seen that Frankie bloke arriving in the club with a blonde girl who was even prettier than Carrie and they went straight to the VIP room and he'd hardly even spoken to her at all! Frankie hasn't rang Carrie for about a week. He seemed to go quiet the moment Carrie said she was staying in Ibiza, a bit like he thought she was coming on too heavy with him. He's a bit of a player if you ask me but Carrie just can't see it. Anyway Carrie was really sobbing and Rodriguez said he didn't want to hear her personal problems and he especially didn't want to bloody hear about Frankie because every girl in that villa had been out with Frankie and he was sick of hearing about him. THEN HE FIRED CARRIE TOO.

We've just moved our things to this youth hostel in the West End of San Antonio and we're looking for new jobs tomorrow. Carrie is quite emotional tonight but I've told her to calm down and get some sleep 'cos we're better off out of there. This is just the start of the adventure.

JULY

THURSDAY 1ST JULY

4pm – San Antonio – Hostal Anibal – Room 337.

See, I knew we could get other jobs! There's loads of
jobs in Ibiza you just have to be determined and blag
yourself into them. I think Uma would be quite proud of
me really. Me and Carrie have got jobs working as
promotion girls at The Magic Parrot which is a bar we
used to go to with Kezia and Uma. Basically we have to
glam ourselves up and stand in the middle of one of the
main streets of the West End of San Antonio from about
9pm to 3am every morning, and try and round up gangs
of boys and girls and drag them into the bar. We get paid
three euros for every group of people we bring in. This
sounded like quite a good deal when we agreed to do it,
but it's actually really hard 'cos there are about a
hundred bars on the same street and some of them have
got proper bare choong hilarious boys working for them
who convince every gang of girls to follow them. Me and
Carrie haven't been making much cash at all. Carrie is
better than me 'cos she wears a really short skirt and high
heels and looks totally gorgeous, but she's only good at
flirting for the first few hours then she gets bored and
goes drinking with boys she's just met and spends

whatever euros she's made that night so she's none left for food the next day.

Barney Draper rang her up today and went totally doolally mental at her. Barney says he's cut off Carrie's credit card today 'cos it's up past its £1000 limit and he's just opened the bill and nearly had a heart attack. Barney has told Carrie to get herself back to England now and he's not giving her another penny. He meant it too 'cos Carrie just tried to use it to buy crisps in the supermercado and it got rejected. I asked Carrie if Barney had any news from my mother and Carrie told me that Barney says that my mother is so angry she refuses to speak about the situation. Ha! My mother refusing to speak? I find this very difficult to believe.

Well this has just made me more determined to prove that we can bloody stand on our own two feet. I'm going to try extra hard at work tonight. I'm a bit worried me and Carrie are going to starve. All we've eaten in the last forty-eight hours is a pot of natural Greek yoghurt between two and a small bag of Doritos. All my clothes and bikinis are baggy now and my face is quite thin. My nan would say I look like one of them Ethiopians. OMG I would give my right arm for one of Nan's chicken dinners right now, with the crispy roast potatoes and the soft chicken and the gravy and a chocolate Sara Lee gateau for pudding with extra squirty cream and then maybe another slice of chicken later in a white roll with some mayo in it and OMG I got to stop thinking about this now 'cos my mouth is watering 'cos I'm so hungry.

Anyway, I spent all last night running up and down outside The Magic Parrot, but I still only made twenty euros and then we had to pay the youth hostel fee so we are still skint. It's proper impossible to get more people into the bar. Everyone is so bloody drunk or off their head on drugs when you try to talk to them they're not really listening or they start giving you proper attitude. And there's always fights breaking out and bottles being smashed and the Ibizan police turning up with dogs to break it up. It's quite scary, but y'know, I'm from Essex, I can handle myself. I'm OK.

Why did I never notice any of this going on before? Me and Kez used to just wander right through the middle of it all laughing, but then we were well drunk too. Carrie says we should have half a bottle of vodka each before we go out working and that'll take the edge off it. That's not such a bad idea.

SUNDAY 4TH JULY

The thing my mum always says about booze is, 'Remember, Shiraz, booze in . . . common sense out!' She says that when she's been proper ear-wigging on me and Carrie planning a night out in Ilford and we're trying to work out who's got cash to buy the Smirnoff Ices. 'Oh, off drinking again are we?' she says. 'Well you be careful! Booze in . . . common sense out.'

I ignore quite a lot of what my mother says these days 'cos most of it is just a plan to stop me having fun, but today I'm thinking she might have a point about alcohol. 'Cos yesterday, the minute me and Carrie started necking that Zubrowka vodka stuff (what tastes of curried frog fallopian tube by the way and don't taste any better when it's set on fire), well all our common sense flew out of the window. That's why we're in this mess, we are. Booze. Sometimes I reckon I'd be better off as a nun. It's not like I'd be having to give up my sex life neither.

We inherited the almost full bottle of Zubrowka off these lads from Glasgow who were flying home last night and were just going to chuck it in the bin. Carrie had been getting off with one of them. Actually Carrie had been getting off with two of them. Not at the same time OF COURSE. She ain't that much of a hooch. She was getting off with one lad called Dougie McTails for a couple of days but then she saw him at the beach and she went off him as he was really bloody hairy. Like, oh-my-god orangutan hairy. Like all over his chest and thighs and big tufty bits of hair sprouting out of his shoulders with a bum crack which me and Caz kept calling 'The Bumcrack of Doom' 'cos it looked like bats might live in it. In fact whenever you saw Dougie coming towards you it was well mesmerizing like he was one big mobile Shredded Wheat with a Celtic Football Shirt on.

Carrie was well put off by Dougie's hairiness, so she dumped him and started seeing his mate Grant who was actually quite dull, but Grant's gran had just carked it so he could afford to drive an Audi RS4. Carrie ain't very deep like that when it comes to boys. And she sort of trusts what they say too. I don't trust anything boys say these days. I'd want to see actual evidence of the Audi, like a photo of Grant at least driving the bloody thing. Until then, I'd just assume he was another lying wasteman who went everywhere on the bus. My Wesley weren't like that. He always told the truth.

So, anyway, Carrie turned up back at the youth hostel this afternoon carrying the Zubrowska, looking all tearful, so I said, 'Aw, Carrie, what's up, darling? Are you sad that Grant's gone home?'

Carrie just looks at me funny and said, 'What, oh no, not really. I'm quite relieved to be honest. I couldn't work out a word he was saying half the time, what with his accent. Not being racialist or nothing.'

'So, what's up with your mush then?' I said. 'Oh that dickhead who works at the supermercado has just taken my credit card off me!' moaned Carrie. 'He says the machine told him to do it. I was only trying to buy a packet of Cheetos and some Fanta Limón for our dinner! I was proper pleading with him just to let me keep the card but he starts shouting something at me in Spanish and then he got his bloody dog out of the stock cupboard and it was barking its head off!'

At that point Carrie burst into tears, and they were proper tears too, not the ones she forces out when

Barney says he won't pay for new hair extensions. So we sat on the bed for a bit saying nothing. Carrie's belly was proper grumbling with hunger so I found a tin of old stale Pringles in my suitcase, and we shared a few Gummy Bear jelly sweet things that had been in the room when we got there that weren't that dusty. Then we decided to cheer ourselves up by having some vodka.

We found two little shot glasses and poured some shots and knocked them back quick. It tasted disgusting and made all the hairs stand up on the back of my arms, but within about two minutes, everything seemed a bit brighter. Like the sun was all of a sudden shining and we remembered that this being in Ibiza with no money thing was all an adventure. So then we poured two more shots and clinked glasses and shouted, 'Goodmayes Girls Don't Run, We run Ting!' and we knocked them back and started laughing our heads off. Then we started talking about what we could do to make some money 'cos we needed to eat and pay our hostal bill. Well we decided that the best thing we could do was go to The Magic Parrot early tonight and be properly one hundred per cent assertive and in people's faces and earn as many euros as possible and work until at least 4am.

Carrie agreed to this even though I could see the thought of working hard was making her teeth feel itchy. At one point Carrie started waffling on about that DJ Frankie bloke again and saying she wondered whether he might lend us a bit of money, but I just shook my head at that and tried to change the subject. It's not like Frankie's even looked her way for weeks anyway. We saw him drive by in a car the other day and he didn't even stop.

Anyway, by this point we were pretty drunk. This was definitely 'cos we hadn't really had anything proper to prevent the alcohol reaching our brains so quick. I learned this in Biology at Mayflower. And this was pretty much the ONLY thing I did learn in Biology 'cos I used to sit at the back with Uma and Chantalle Strong and they used to set the school locusts free every week and vandalise the biology textbooks by crossing out the real biology words and writing, 'SPAFF ON HERE' and 'MISS BUNT IZ A BUCKETBLUT' all over them. Then they'd get sent out and I'd get sent with them 'cos I was wearing a hoodie and hoops too.

But in the rare times that I wasn't outside the door I did learn that it's better if you eat before you drink alcohol as it gets in to your bloodstream slower and stops you acting like a schizoid mentaloid in public.

But me and Carrie still had another vodka. And then we had one that we'd set on fire for some reason. And then we borrowed the boys down the corridors' iPod cradle and we had a bit of a dance to some bassline tracks and then we got ready for work and we plastered ourselves in make-up. In fact so MUCH make-up we looked like Sean Burton did when he went to Sonia Cathcart's eighteenth birthday as Christina Aguilera doing *Moulin Rouge*. But by this point we didn't care, 'cos we were raring to get out there and make some cash.

We ran down to work, tripping over each other when we got out on the street, totally giddy. This was obviously proper infectious to the passers-by 'cos we actually started making money by simply grabbing blokes by the arm and FORCING them to drink at The Magic Parrot. But the thing about the job is that you've got to keep your wits about you 'cos you're not meant to encourage total nutters into the bar – nutters who might cause trouble and smash the place up. That is a BIG NO NO.

If me and Cazza hadn't been so plastered out of our heads ourselves, we might have realised that the hen party of about twenty girls from Workington in Cumbria that we bumped into were maybe gonna be TROUBLE.

I mean, our first warning might have been that they were practically the most naked girls we had ever seen who were dressed to go out. Ever! All they had on were fluffy bikini tops, devil horns, and rubber hot pants. And I'm not being funny but some of them were a bit too large for their rubber hot pants 'cos there was serious camel-toe action going on, and their boobs were all hanging out of their bikini tops, like they were making an escape for freedom. It was sort of bleak to look at. A bit like at school when Latoya Bell used to roll her school skirt up and parade about with the bottoms of her bum cheeks hanging out with all cellulite on them and the odd spot. Sometimes 'less is more', innit?

Anyway, you'd think me and Carrie might have

noticed that one of the Workington girls was wearing a policeman's hat that looked totally real like she'd just STOLEN it off someone's head. And you'd think alarm bells might have gone off when the only reason we noticed these girls was 'cos one of them was on the ground outside The Magic Parrot challenging some random geezer she'd met to a press-up competition which she was winning NO PROBLEM, even though she was doing it with a fag in her gob while her friend was holding her kebab!

But OH NO, me and Carrie didn't notice any of that, all we noticed was that there were about twenty of them and we could earn some serious euros by getting them inside the bar.

So we dragged them into The Magic Parrot with the promise of free Tequila shots and 'an exciting pole dancing competition with big cash prizes' and pretty soon the whole mob of them were downstairs making a right old noise and within about five minutes some woman from Huddersfield was shouting at one of them, 'Oh, you! Bitch! Get your hands off my boyfriend's tackle! I'll smack your teeth out!' And the hen party girls were all shouting back, 'Oh chill out you miserable cow! Anyway we thought he was your son, you're so bloody old and wrinkly!' And then someone threw a whole glass of a cocktail over Huddersfield woman's dress and she went mental screaming and she had about ten mates with her and then a table got kicked over and glasses were smashing and a chair was thrown and then it ALL KICKED OFF.

There was about thirty-five British women – all in hotpants and Morgan De Toi mini-dresses and stack-heeled sandals – slapping each other and getting dragged outside by the bouncers. There was fake chicken fillet boobs flying everywhere and clumps of hair on the floor and Carrie stood somewhere in the middle shouting, 'Oh, for God's sake stop it, you silly cows! STOP IT!!' Well the girl who'd been doing the press-ups, took proper offence to that and smacked Carrie one right across the face and Carrie fell over backwards and was out cold unconscious. It was horrible. I thought she could be dead.

On the bright side, this seemed to stop the fighting 'cos Carrie was just lying there not moving and all the girls were crowding around and one was screaming, 'Don't move her! Don't move her! She might have broken her back!'

I was totally frozen to the spot just opening and closing my mouth, but then as I finally ran forward to try to take charge, Carrie started to sit up. THANK GOD!!! But I was worried she might have a head injury so I still had to take her to San Antonio Emergency Room. And we waited for hours and hours and the nurses were just as moody and they got out Carrie's medical files from a few weeks ago, when she fell off the booze cruise boat and drank the sewage. Then they pretended not to speak

English for the rest of the night. In fact the only English we heard for the next eight hours was when Luka, who owns The Magic Parrot, called Carrie to say that on account of the smashed chairs and the broken glasses we were both FIRED and we should never darken his doors ever again.

MONDAY 5TH JULY

To – theshizzlebizzle@hotmail.com
From – uma.bruntonfletch@virginmedia.com
Subject: HOW ARE YOU?

Hello Shiz, it's Uma. You OK, babe? I wish you'd ring me and tell me if everything is good. I'm worried about you, Shiz. Look, sorry for being a stress head on the last day before I went home, right? I know it was bare childish of me to get on the coach and not say a proper goodbye, but to be totally straight up, Shizzlebizzle, I was angry with you and I could feel my head proper starting to fizz and feel a bit mental just like it did in Year 8 before I locked Mr Angus inside the art room kiln thing that they bake pots in for eleven hours after he gave me that D minus for my pottery. Y'know, when my anger sort of takes over, yagetme?

The thing is, Shiz, the one thing I learned from the counsellers at pupil referral unit is that I must manage my anger and notice the signs of it rising. So when you said you were deffo one hundred per cent not changing your mind about coming home and staying in Ibiza with Carrie (who sometimes I reckon has a bloody screw loose. Not being funny or nothing 'cos me and her have been mates since back in the day and I love her to bits, but I do sometimes think she's nuts, Shiz) well, I was proper LIVID. So I decided to get on the coach and think about something calmer that would put me in a 'good place'. In fact, I imagined that happy bit at the end of *Monsters Inc*. when Sulley gets reunited with Boo, then before I knew it I was feeling more chilled out and the bus was at the airport and I was on the plane home.

I'm sorry, Shiz. I was only being narky 'cos I was worried something bad might happen to you over there on your own which I'm sure it won't 'cos you're not an idiot, even if Carrie is. Bloody hell, Shiz, don't bloody show Carrie this email or she'll do one of her fake crying sessions for the rest of the day like she did that time Kezia told her she had wonky tits. LMAO!!!

Anyway, me and Kez got home in one piece. Kez ain't been too well since we got home, she says. She's got stomach pains and she's going up Dr Gupta tomorrow to get checked out for food poisoning. Saying that, I saw her eat Honey Nut Loops out of a box with dead ants in it, so it ain't out of the question, innit?

I'm still in Whitechapel at the moment but I'm getting my new flat in west London any day soon. I went to check it out the other day with Mr Deng. It was well POSH, Shiraz. I got my own room and it's proper clean and quiet and it's got a little shower room all of its own and the kitchen is white and new! You've gotta come and see me there, blud! I am a LADY now. (Ha ha ha, not really, I'm still just me.) But honest to God, Shiz, my Zeus is going to love it 'cos there's a park right near by for his walks. Oh and by the way, Zeus could do with some long walks at the moment. I came home to find that your mother has fed him till he's the size of a racehorse! He looked proper disappointed when I went to pick him up from 34 Thundersley Road. Your mum said he has grown quite accustomed to his eleven o'clock Greggs iced doughnut, and his before bedtime chunky KitKat. Your Pen weren't exactly looking any more Slimline, either. HA HA HA too jokes.

Oh, and by the way, Shiz, I saw your Wesley Barington Bains II last week when I was in Goodmayes. I saw him in The Litten Tree pub. It was 'Beer and a curry for a fiver' night down there and he was stood at the bar when I went in. He was with that Sooz girl with the frizzmop hair who always has a mush on her like she's on her period. Well, I think Wes must've been on his period too 'cos honest to God, Shiz, he had a face like a dropped pie. Proper sour he was.

So when Sooz goes to the loo, Wesley asks me about you. Where you were and that. So I told him you'd stayed on in Ibiza and had no plans for coming home right now and he looked well narked. Then he didn't say much else. He just ordered a single malt whiskey to go with his lager as a chaser and he knocked that back in one. I dunno what that means, Shiz. Maybe he's turning into an alco? Saying that, being stuck in the house all day with Little Miss Smile-a-While, would make anyone hit the bottle, innit? Anyway, I won't go on about Wesley. He's not your bloody problem any more is he? OK, Shizza, got to go. I hope you pick up this mail. I miss you lots. WRITE BACK, YOU, AND TELL ME YOU'RE OK, YOU ANNOYING BLOODY BINT.

GOODMAYES GIRLS RUN TING 4EVER – UmaBFxxx

TUESDAY 6TH JULY

The thing about me, Shiraz Bailey Wood, is that I'm one of life's survivors. I just am, believe me. And I didn't used to think this at all, I used to think I was proper unlucky, but these days I've got a bit more faith that everything's gonna be OK and someone really is looking after me. I ain't worked out who that is yet, though. I dunno whether it's God or Allah or that bloke in the spaceship that Marsha Boyd at Mayflower School's mum and dad used to believe in. Scientologists, they were called. Like Tom Cruise! That was bare jokes 'cos the Boyds, they didn't look like A-list celebrities at all, in fact her dad used to drive a burgundy Hyundai Pony, and her mum used to wear Matalan sweat-suits and sit outside Ilford Xchange on deck chairs trying to offer folk 'stress tests'. Turns out that this is what Scientologists do to get people into their religion. I never fancied it myself.

To be honest though, if I'm going to be taken over by religion one day I'm hoping I turn out to be Jewish 'cos I used to sit next to Sophia Weinberg in the canteen when

I worked at House of Hardy and her packed lunch always looked AMAZING. You have to love a God what's into smoked salmon sandwiches with spready cheese and home made chicken soup, innit?

I was just telling Carrie all of this just now but she wasn't listening to me as she is in the pits of despair what with her bruised face and bloodshot eye.

So after about twenty minutes of me having a one-woman conversation about God, the universe and all that sort of thing, Cazza sits up in bed and yells, 'Shizzle what the hell are you chatting about now, you nutjob?'

'I was just saying, Carrie,' I said, 'that I sometimes wonder if there is a mysterious power at work up above. Like today when I walked past that Fever nightclub just at the moment when this geezer was putting up a poster next door to it that looked very much like a job advert. What were the chances of that, eh?'

'Mmmmm,' she says, not looking overtaken by the holy spirit at all.

Anyway, so when I saw the poster, I stopped the guy sticking it up and goes, '*Buenos Dias!* Job? *'Por favor?* Yes!? Job here? Today!?' And he grunted at me and eventually said, 'Yes, go see Aldo.' So I wandered into Fever and went to the back office and found the manager Aldo and he spoke quite good English and I turned on the full Shiraz Bailey Wood charm which has got me many, many jobs over the last few years and, well, the long and short of it is that me and Carrie now have new jobs collecting glasses at EUROPE'S MOST FAMOUS FOAM PARTY! Woot woooooot woooot! Brappppage x gazillion!!! We begin tomorrow night!! And we get paid cash in hand at the end of the shift! Praise be! Allah is wise!

So I wiffled on for a bit longer tonight telling Carrie why we are so lucky and why everything is going to be great and after a bit Carrie sighed and rearranged the ice-cube pack on her swollen face and said, 'Seriously, Shiz, I sort of see what you're saying. But I just think that if this is all down to God, I reckon he's looking down at us right now and having a good old laugh at my expense.'

THURSDAY 8TH JULY

We've just done our first Fever Foam Party. It was OK. Not bad at all really. Most importantly, me and Caz made enough euros to pay our youth hostel bill and buy some food. So we're still here, we're doing OK, WE'RE STILL ROCKING! Oh yes, it takes more than being fired twice, a bar brawl and three days living on half a packet of second hand Gummy Bears to crush the Goodmayes Girls' spirit!!! Shiz and Carrie don't run, we run ting, innit! OH MY DAYZZZZZZZ I have been in this type of mood all day. I am proper giddy. I am high on life. Carrie reckons it's 'cos I've only eaten about 250 calories since June and now I've just blown all what's left of my wages on Coca-cola, chocolate and a massive bag of sherbert flying saucers. Carrie says I'm just buzzing on all the sugar and that when I come down off this 'rush' I'm going to realise that glass collecting at Fever is probably the worst job in the history of jobs EVER. Carrie says that filling a nightclub with foam for people to dance through is totally sad and 'a bit 1990s' and that's why she said NO to Barney when he wanted to do it in Time and Envy in Romford for her Super Sweet Sixteen party. Carrie also said that she's pretty sure that the foam Aldo is using when he fills the nightclub ain't the official foam you're meant to use 'cos it's irritating her throat and eyes, what with her having very sensitive skin and lungs.

'Look, bruv,' I said to her. 'You were hardly IN the foam! You were standing at the bar giggling at every bloody word the bartender Sergio said and getting him to give you free shots of Sambuca.' Carrie ignored that bit and just said that she reckons there's probably all manner of air-bound viruses floating about in the foam and the fact that all the club goers go MENTALOID when the foam starts squirting out of the machine and start snogging each other and feeling each other up and stripping off their clothes and doing ALL SORTS OF BLOODY THINGS they think no one can see 'cos the foam makes them invisible, well that just makes the germs worse. Carrie is well scared she might get that Bird Flu Virus thing she once saw on the news. Carrie told all of this to Aldo and she's told him she needs some sort of germ mask and a pair of large tweezers to pick up all the leftover underwear on the dancefloor at the end of the night 'cos she ain't faffing about with anyone's skiddie undies for any amount of Euros. Apparently Aldo told her that he would 'get back to her'. I dunno what she's bloody complaining about, I think the job is OK. I mean it's a job, innit? It's keeping us here in Ibiza, and we can buy food! To be honest I can't write any more now 'cos I think I am at the peak of my sugar rush. I've got a pain above one eye and my heart is proper bumping and I'm sweating a sort of cold sweat. But apart from that I feel BLOODY GREAT.

FRIDAY 9TH JULY

OK, so tonight was a bit grim. Plus Aldo went missing at the end of the night so we didn't get our wages. Now I've got to go and track him down somewhere in the West End in one of his many nightclubs and bars which is a bit of a balls-ache as I wanted to go to the internet café today. I've not checked my email for weeks. It's proper expensive doing it all the time and to be totally honest, since Wesley sent me that email saying he didn't want me no more, well I sort of stopped wanting to know about Goodmayes. I don't want to think about Essex and the mess I've made of everything at home.

I've got to accept that Wes is happy now and he's not thinking about me at all. I know he's probably a lot happier with Sooz than he was with me 'cos at least Sooz knows where her life's going and Sooz has got a proper job at Boots where she starts at 9am every day and wears a white coat and does something useful. She's not Shiraz Bailey Wood who starts work at 2am and wears cut off denims and spends the night feeling her way about in a cloud of foam, coughing her guts up and tripping over people who are actually DOING IT right there in the foam!! And then, at the end of the night, I have to wander about with a black bin liner, wearing big yellow plastic gloves and pick up all the leftover rubbish.

Today I found:

Two bikini tops.

Four Thongs.

One pair of underpants (and not lemon fresh ones, BELIEVE ME).

One River Island patent stiletto.

One inflatable sheep.

One big pair of size 22 Marks and Spencer Magic Support Knickers.

One condom – USED.

One girl, aged 22, from Cleethorpes, called Julie who had fallen asleep behind the foam machine.

Five piles of vomit in various colours, shapes and textures.

Oh and worst of all . . . one poo.

No honestly. A human poo. A little curled up one, just sitting there by the DJ Booth. HOW? Who does a poo on a nightclub dancefloor? Who gets so over-excited when they're out clubbing that they think, 'Oh I'll just drop me pants and squeeze one out here on the floor'??? WHY ARE PEOPLE SO MINGING????!!! So I went and told Aldo and he just grunted at me to go and find the dustpan and brush and get on with removing it. OH MY GOD, IT WAS DISGUSTING.

I haven't told Carrie about the poo. I don't think she could cope with it. I don't think Carrie even does her own poos. And if she does I reckon it's just once a month and they're tiny, pink pellets that look and smell like strawberry bon-bons. Got to go now, need to find Aldo and get paid.

To: theshizzlebizzle@hotmail.com
From: discodanny1million@hotmail.com

Look, Shizza, ARE YOU PICKING UP THESE MAILS OR WHAT LOVE??? This is the third one I've sent and you're not replying, you rude cow! Me and Sean are hoping it's 'cos you're having too much of an AMAZING time, but it just ain't like you not to stay in touch. Carrie's phone doesn't seem to be working either. Send me some evidence to say you're alive, Shiraz. I don't want to worry like an old woman but you know what I'm like. Last time I saw you, you were in Arrival, you'd painted your boobs green and were doing the Macarena. That was the last I heard of you.

Look, I'll be here all day at my desk and I'm going to check my inbox every half hour. If you send me a message I'll mail you back and we can go on MSN. Sean sends his love by the way. He's really good. He's looking into courses to become a fashion designer at the moment. I encouraged him to put his talent to good use. He's still sewing sequins and extra buttons on to everything he can get his hands on – like you said he did in Sixth Form at Mayflower Academy! I'm sitting here at Working Magic wearing trousers with glitter zips. How they've not worked out here that I'm gay is HYSTERICAL. My manager, Precious, who is from Botswana brought in a photo of her daughter yesterday who lives back home and tried to fix me up!! HA HA HA. Honest, Shiz, if I weren't gay then I would have turned it anyway. I thought it was a picture of the tribal goat. I told Precious I am practically spoken for now and she sulked for the next two hours and . . . actually, Shiz, this is just another email you won't read so I'm stopping writing now.

GET IN TOUCH, FIERCE GIRL!!

Dannyxxxxxxxx

SUNDAY 11TH JULY

OH MY GOD. We appear to have been 'let go' from Fever. We don't work there no more. We ain't been fired, OH NO. It's just that Aldo has suddenly realised he has 'too many staff' so he is 'giving us the chance to make more money elsewhere 'cos he won't have any shifts for us'. I might have believed him a bit more if me and Carrie hadn't bumped into SIX POLISH GIRLS we'd never seen before just as we were leaving his office, who were clocking on for work. They all had big smiles on their faces and looked all enthusiastic and raring to go like they couldn't bloody wait to wrestle a human poo on to a dustpan with a spatula and handle smeggy pants.

So then Carrie goes over to Sergio who works behind the bar and shouts, 'Oi, Sergio! I've been given the push! I don't work here no more!' And Sergio just looks at her funny and says, 'What? You worked here!? I thought you were just here on holiday with your friends! I've never seen you pick up a glass ever! Ha ha ha ha!' Carrie got the right hump at that and told him to 'go shag himself'. I linked arms with her then and dragged her out of Fever and we went for a walk on the sea front near Café Mambo and Café Del Mar. We spent our wages on a cheap pizza and a can of lager and we sat on a wall and ate it while watching all the kids who've just got here on holiday going out for the night looking all happy like they didn't have a single care in the world.

The thing I've not told Carrie is that I asked Aldo if he knew anywhere else with jobs going and he gave me the name of a place that definitely had. So I rang them tonight and it's sounding like we'll end up doing it. I've just not told Carrie yet 'cos she's not going to like it at all.

Not one little bit.

WEDNESDAY 14TH JULY

Oh my God. OH MY GOD. Oh my God. OH my God. NO
NO NO NO NO NO NO NO NO NOOOOOOOOOOO
OOOOOO NO NO NO NO NO!!

THURSDAY 15TH JULY

I am well worried about Carrie 'cos she appears to have
stopped speaking and withdrawn into herself completely
on account of our new employment. I was totally right
about Carrie not being a poo-friendly type of person.
And the same goes for wees and tampon inner tubes and
now I come to think of it most things to do with toilets,
which is why being a toilet attendant is not really bringing
out the best in her, even if the tips are bare good and
we're richer than we've been for weeks. 'Cos most of the
girls who come into the loos at Spaceship nightclub –
which begins at 10am in the morning and goes on all day
long – are totally munted off their heads on either Es or
ketamine and when they're not trying to hitch up their
dresses and wee in the sink, 'cos they 'can't be arsed with
the queue', they're trying to hug you and tell you they
love you or get your email address so you can be
bridesmaid at their wedding and then they give you a one
euro tip!

Me and Carrie have to wear big blue plasticky
cleaner's coats and long yellow gloves and white wellies

and white hair nets and every half hour we have to slosh out the loos with mops and buckets of disinfectant, and GOD KNOWS, I try to cheer Carrie up by doing a little dance with my mop and bucket and singing my 'Flying Without Wings' by Westlife every time we find a sanitary towel with wings on the floor, but today this just made Carrie even sadder. In fact today, the only thing Carrie said all shift was, 'I WISH TO GOD THAT EVERYONE'S POOS WOULD PLEASE STOP RE-APPEARING AFTER THEY'VE FLUSHED THEM!! AAAAAAAAAAAAAGH, I CAN'T TAKE IT NO MORE!!!!'

Then Carrie went and locked herself in the cleaners supply cupboard and wouldn't come out until I'd persuaded Rosa, who usually cleans the sinks and sells people squirts of perfume and lollipops, to swap places with her. I reckon Carrie's got to pull herself together. I know it is the most revolting job ever but we're actually on to a good thing here as toilet cleaners. The tips are good and you meet nice people and best of all no other girl on the entire island wants to do it so we can't get fired for at least a week.

SUNDAY 18TH JULY

Carrie had a right face on her today. Carrie says this Ibiza trip hasn't worked out anything like she expected it to 'cos she never in a million years thought she'd end up with her arm down a toilet trying to unblock it with an unravelled coat hanger. Carrie says she's dying to ring her dad and get him to fly us both out of here 'cos she is in hell, but she's not bloody going to on account of how totally RUDE he was last time she called him asking for cash.

Carrie claims that she's not ringing her dad EVER AGAIN because it's the worst thing she could do to Barney, to stop calling altogether. 'Cos then his mind will work overtime and he'll imagine she's been sold as a sex slave in Morroco and this will drive him mental and totally teach him for switching off her Platinum Mastercard when he knew full well how important that card was to her and how it 'gave her confidence' and a 'sense of independence'. And now the mean old git has stripped away all of who she is and she hopes he's bloody happy.

Basically Carrie has whinged on like a spoilt brat for ages all the way home from Spaceship and I was just about to tell her to bloody shut up when this Jeep pulls up beside us with blackened windows and the window rolls down and Carrie's face just lit up with happiness 'cos it was Frankie. He was by himself, no weirdo mates for once.

So Frankie says, 'Carrie baby! I thought it was you. You're looking beautiful as ever, darling. How's it going!?' 'Oh things are great, Frankie,' Carrie said. 'We've just been partying down at Spaceship! That place is amazing isn't it?'

And Frankie says, 'Yeah, I play there sometimes. I used

to have a residency there but now I like to have the freedom to play where I want.'

Well Carrie clearly thought this was well cool 'cos she was fluttering her eyelids at him and twirling her hair. I was dying to say, ''Ere, Frankie, why do you never actually seem to play a set anywhere? In fact all you do is talk about it. My mate Uma thinks you're shady as hell.' But I didn't say that of course, 'cos to be honest Frankie is rather scary.

So then Frankie asked for Carrie's phone number again, which he claimed to have lost, and said he would give her a bell as he'd love to 'hang' with her soon. And then he drove off and Carrie stood there looking like she'd necked six pills of whatever that stuff is that people take in Spaceship, 'cos she floated up the road with a big grin on her mush, giggling all the way home.

MONDAY 19TH JULY

3pm – San Antonio – Hostal Anibal – Room 337.

I'm not sure how much longer me and Carrie are going to live in the youth hostel. It's proper cheap and everything and quite clean but me and Caz have had a room for three people to ourselves so far and today another girl has moved in. She was a dancer at Arrival until yesterday, but she's just been kicked out of the Villa Los Antilles too. We don't quite know why. Proper paranoid she is. I asked her what her name is and she said, 'I'm not telling you. You'll tell them. Shhhh they can hear you!' So I said to her, 'Who can?' and she said, 'Stop it! Stop trying to fool me!' Then she got all of her make-up out of her bag and lined it up in dead straight lines. Her name is Gabriella Diaz and she's from Barcelona. I only know this as she left her passport on her bed when she went to the loo. She's a size 0 and her skin is really pale, the colour of when my nan makes porridge, and she cries a lot. On balance I think I preferred living with the tampon-in-teacup woman.

TUESDAY 20TH JULY

6pm – Carrie is very very giddy today 'cos Frankie rang her last night. Carrie's acting like a different girl now, like someone just switched her on at the back again!

'I knew he'd start missing me soon. We've got a connection me and him!' Carrie keeps saying.

Frankie says that girl that he was with in Arrival wasn't a date or anything, it was his mate's sister. Frankie says he's sorry he's not been around to take Carrie out or anything but he was back in Kent over the last few days looking after some business. Carrie says that now that Frankie is back in Ibiza he wants to take her out for a posh dinner tonight.

Carrie has been planning her outfit and scrubbing dead skin off her heels and plucking her eyebrows all day. Carrie says I've got to tell the Spaceship people that she's come down with a sudden mystery vomiting bug and that she won't be coming to work this evening. Carrie says that Frankie says that the plan is that Carrie has got to get ready and make herself as 'stunning as she always is', then do Frankie a favour and get a taxi to Evissa airport, pick up a record box full of records that Frankie is having imported, then get a taxi up to his villa in the hills near Playa Del Bossa. Then once she's brought him the record box, Carrie and Frankie can go out for dinner. Apparently Frankie is really excited about it 'cos he's totally missed having her around.

Personally I think Frankie's got a bloody cheek, ignoring Carrie for weeks and then having her doing favours for him, but I'm not saying nothing 'cos Carrie is really happy today and hasn't cried once. I just hope Carrie brings a doggie bag back from her posh dinner. I'd eat anything right now. ANYTHING. I'd even eat a depressed lobster that's just had its head smacked in with a hammer. I'd probably eat one of my mother's yummy elastoplast and Cif lemon cleaner Sunday bloody dinners. I'd probably eat my own bum in a baguette if it had enough tomato sauce on it. I am bloody totally starving.

WEDNESDAY 21ST JULY

Carrie didn't come home today. Not at all. I'm trying not to get all mad at her or nothing but I hope she's not going to bloody drop me like this for the rest of the adventure or I will be livid. It wouldn't exactly be the first time she's dropped me in favour of a boy. She's been doing it since Year 7. Yeah, Carrie. This is true. But you always come crawling back, don't you though, when it all goes tits up and you need someone who can make you laugh. Someone who can make you laugh by, say, by doing her impression of Sonia Cathcart running about with a burning bumbag going, 'Jeeeeeeesus Christ save meeeeeeee! Save meeeeeeee my fanny is on fire!!' Or by doing her impression of Bart Simpson touching himself up shouting, 'Cowabunga Dude!!' You don't get boyfriends that can make you laugh like that, DO YOU?!

The thing is I'm not bothered if Carrie wants to go off with Frankie and be all madly in love 'cos it's not like I don't know a few people around here I can chat to and that, but it's when she just disappears and leaves me clueless where she is that it does my head in. Anyway, I'm off to work now and I'm not going to worry about her any more. I'm not her bloody mother, am I?

THURSDAY 22ND JULY

Oh my God.

None of this seems real. It's like a bloody nightmare that I can't wake up from. I can't write anything proper today even if this is the bit the film director who makes the film of my diary will really need to know all about. I just can't write anything else, so whoever is reading this, I'm well sorry. I just don't know what to do. I just don't know what to do.

FRIDAY 23RD JULY

OK, right, Carrie is in prison. She was arrested on Tuesday night getting out of a taxi and walking into Frankie's villa by a load of police who claim she was smuggling drugs on to the island. Carrie was NOT smuggling drugs on to the island! Carrie doesn't bloody take drugs and she isn't a drug dealer! She was tricked by that horrible nasty piece of rubbish Frankie into picking up that record box for him. And it wasn't just a box of records at all. There was a big bag of ecstasy pills in there too. I can't bloody believe she could be so stupid. And why the hell did I let her go and do it?! Me and Caz watch *CSI Miami* every week and we're always laughing at retards who get fooled into doing stuff like this. I mean, why would Frankie need a box of records? We've never seen him play one single set since we got here.

Apparently Frankie has been arrested, too, and so has Marcellus and so has Terry, the one that looks like a bear who Carrie made me go out to dinner with. I hope they lock them in a box and throw away the key. Oh God, I hope they don't do that to Carrie though.

I found out about Caz yesterday night when I got to

146

work at Spaceship. All the British people who work in the bars in the West End are talking about it. I couldn't stop crying when I heard, so Stella and Jody the barmaids kept giving me free vodkas but that just made me cry more. People keep saying Carrie will get four years in Ibizan prison. FOUR WHOLE YEARS. That's like spending all the way from Year 7 at school right through to Year 10 sitting in the same room including all the school holidays. I feel sick just thinking about it. Carrie will do something stupid. She hates small spaces. I am so worried about her and there's nothing I can do.

I went up to the police station first thing this morning but I don't speak any Spanish and there was no one there who spoke English, or so they reckoned anyway. So I kept saying, 'CARRIE DRAPER' really loudly and they kept saying, 'Manyana, Manyana.'

But eventually, after I cried like a nutjob for about twenty minutes, another policeman who was just walking past said, 'Tomorrow. My colleague is saying tomorrow. Your friend is in the cells. British Consulate come tomorrow and speak to her. No visitors until tomorrow.'

I think I've heard of this British Consulate bloke on the news before. I think he's the man who can sort it all out. I hope so. I couldn't go to work tonight 'cos I got back too late so now I've hardly got any money at all. Gabriella my roommate had to give me three euros for the bus to the police station and then I had nothing left for any dinner. I'm hoping manyana might be better. I'm going to shut my eyes now and when I wake up I'm hoping it will all be over.

SATURDAY 24TH JULY

I got up this morning at 8am 'cos the sun was shining through the window of our room. Gabriella was out raving with these Portugese guys she met this week, no doubt making her loopy paranoid delusional problems much worse with another round of ketamine and coke, but I'm not worrying for Gabriella. I can't deal with her problems too. So I got dressed in my pink trackie bottoms and bikini top and put on my little TopShop T-shirt which all smell funny and are far too big for me 'cos my bum and boobs have shrunk to nothing due to lack of food. I put on my gold hoops and flip flops then I set off walking the mile or so through San Antonio to the police station. San Antonio looks like a bomb has dropped at that time in the morning. There was vomit and smashed glass everywhere and kids lying on the pavement crashed-out asleep who I had to keep stepping over as I walked along. I was proper sweaty and tired by the time I got there. When I walked through the police station doors the same geezers were on the front desk as yesterday but they were a bit more friendly to me this time 'cos I'd asked Gabriella to teach me a few words of Spanish so at least I could say, 'I am here to see my friend' and 'I'm sorry I don't speak much Spanish.'

Well this seemed to warm them up a lot, in fact they started trying to help me then which made me feel like crying 'cos it reminded me of how Uma taught me that trick when she learned Cantonese. I miss Uma so much and I wish I'd bloody listened to her and hadn't stayed in Ibiza, but as I always say, there ain't no time for regrets in this life. That's what people like Beyoncé and Mariah Carey say in their songs, you've just got to keep your head held high and keep reaching for the sky and all that sort of crap that divas sing while throwing their hair about. It helps in life if you think like that. Sort of.

Well I waited and I waited and I waited and I waited and I waited in this horrible smelly waiting room with nothing to read aside from a leaflet someone had left about that bloody parrot park that Billy Big Gob the holiday rep tried to sell us tickets to with an actual picture of the parrot on the little bike and believe me it didn't look like it was having a good time. In fact I was wondering whether its feet were blu-tacked to the handlebars 'cos it didn't look like it was enjoying the ride at all . . . And then my mind wandered and I started imagining what the parrot would taste like with all its feathers off and done for about eight minutes in a George Foreman Lean Mean Grilling Machine with maybe a bit of HP Barbecue Sauce on it, put in a floury bap straight off the shelf all warm from ASDA bakery because I hadn't eaten for days and by this point I think

I was starting to hallucinate. Then one of the policeman came and proper poked me in the shoulder and said, 'You see your friend now.'

The policeman took me through a big, thick door and down a set of stairs and along a long corridor and into another room and I had to get full-body searched by a grumpy woman with moles on her chin with hair sprouting out of them and then I was allowed into the next room which just had a desk in it and a phone sitting beside a glass window.

Well I didn't really understand what was going on then and the woman just sort of growled something in Spanish and then shoved me through the door and locked it behind me.

So I walked up to where the phone was and looked through the window and that's when I saw her. Carrie. Sitting there staring back through the window at me. She looked awful. Tiny and knackered and ill. And I was staring at her thinking, 'What's different about you?' and then I realised that she had no gold earrings on and no make-up on and I don't think I ever saw Carrie without a bit of gold and at least her Maybelline mascara since Year 6 Primary Class. I thought I might start crying when I saw her but I didn't 'cos I was totally shocked and numb and Carrie didn't cry neither, well 'cept for one little tear, which she wiped on her horrible Spanish prison hoodie that they'd given her to wear that looked all stained like a crack-head had given birth on it or something. So I picked up the phone and said, 'All right, darling, how's it going?'

And Carrie picks up hers and says, 'Well, Shizzlebizzle, I've been on better dates.'

And I sort of laughed but it wasn't at all funny and then we sat looking at each other saying nothing and I said, 'What does that Spanish Consulate bloke say? Can he get you out of here?'

Carrie just sighed and says, 'I don't think it really works like that, Shiz. He's been in touch with my dad and told him what the police case is against me so he can get a lawyer, but that's it really. I think he was flying out last night. I ain't spoken to my parents. I was only allowed one phone call on Tuesday night so I called Draperville and they were both at my dad's golf club dinner so I told Mrs Raziq and she went proper hysterical, and then Molechin there took the phone off me.'

Well as Carrie was saying this, Molechin wanders back into my side of the room and starts grumbling on in Spanish and tapping her watch so I knew I was going to get slung out soon. So then Carrie says, 'Shiz, why are you still in Ibiza?'

'I'm here to help you, you total nutbag, why do you think?' I said.

But Carrie looked very sad. 'You should just go home, Shizzle. Don't stay here for me, I ain't getting out of here for ages. Years maybe.'

It was weird when she said 'years' 'cos she didn't even look scared or anything, her eyes were just proper blank and red-rimmed. I didn't tell Carrie that even if I wanted to go home I can't afford a ticket. I went into a travel bureau yesterday and asked how much a flight to London would be and they said that it was peak season now and the cheapest they could sell me was 700 euros. Well I haven't even got seven euros. I didn't tell Carrie that. I didn't want her to worry.

So then Carrie sat staring at her nails, which were all bitten with chipped pink nail-varnish on them, and she says, 'I keep asking them when the woman who does the manicures arrives but they don't seem to understand what I mean.'

I tried to laugh at that but my throat seemed to be closing up.

Then a policewoman appeared on Carrie's side and starts taking the phone out of her hand and Carrie pulls it back and says, 'Look I gotta go, Shiz. Remember this right, I love you to bits. You're my bezzie and I won't forget about you right? Keep it real, Shiz, eh?'

And I started crying then and I said, 'Yeah, keep it real, Cazza.'

And then they turned the phones off and took Carrie away and shut the door.

So I walked back up the stairs and out of the police station and my head's racing like I'm tripping out of my nut or something and I stumble out of the doors into the fresh air and then next thing I knew I bump slap bang right into this man coming the opposite way. Well I straighten myself up and look at him properly and it's Barney Draper! Carrie's dad. Standing right there in front of me. And he's just staring at me and his face starts turning really angry and scary like I've never seen him look before and he then he starts shouting. He's proper going off his head going, 'Shiraz, what the bloody hell has been going on? I thought you had some sense! How could you let this happen! That's my little girl in there! She's going to be rotting away in a Spanish prison!'

Well I tried to speak to him but I could see he was just as freaked out as I was and I don't know if he meant all the horrible things he said after that but in the end he told me to get out of his sight 'cos he couldn't look at me. So I did. I just ran away.

I headed back in the direction of the youth hostel and I was sort of in another world by now. My flip flops were rubbing blisters between my toes and I think I'd went over on my ankle at some point 'cos it was hurting and I was trying my best to work out what to do next. Somehow I ended up in the internet café and the girls that run it gave me a coffee and let me have a free fifteen minute credit. I checked my emails and there was one from my mother who knew all about Carrie saying how angry and upset and worried she was about me out there in Ibiza and that they don't know what they can do to get me home as they haven't got any money and neither has Nan and Clement. Mum said Murphy and Cava-Sue were down at Cash Converters right then selling everything they could get their hands on but she still didn't think it was nearly enough for a ticket home. She said she'd mail me again soon, but then my credit was up and I left as I didn't want the girls to think I was hanging about looking for more freebies 'cos I've still got my pride.

So I came back to my room and I'm lying on my bed now and I'm really really trying to think what to do next but just for now I'm going to put this diary back in my suitcase and wrap my arms around my legs and curl up in a little ball and try and go to sleep. This feels like the end of the world.

SUNDAY 25TH JULY

I'll never forget this day for the rest of my life.

I woke up this morning and when I opened my eyes it took about one whole minute before I remembered what had happened. It was the best minute I've had for days. Then it all came back to me again and I got up really quickly and got dressed before all the horrible thoughts about Carrie in her little cell came flooding over me again. I left the youth hostel and walked down towards the beach and sat on a lounger for a bit facing the sea watching all the holiday makers go off sunbathing and I thought about me and Uma and Kezia and how amazing our holiday had been – and how long ago that was. Then a bloke turned up and wanted some euros for me to sit there so I had to go. Then I walked back slowly by Los Paradiso apartments and I could hear Billy Big Gob in the bar downstairs selling his trips to the botanical garden then I walked past the karaoke bar where Carrie won all of her money for singing so badly and then I walked past the little café where me and Kez used to always get egg and chips on the way home when we'd been out boozing. And just at that moment I realised that I was standing in the middle of the street in a foreign country thousands of miles from home with about two quid in my pocket and no ticket to get home and no friends and no plan for my destiny. And right then I sort of gave up any hope. I started feeling totally paranoid and shaky. Probably like Gabriella feels most of the time, poor cow. That's what I felt like. Like people in the shops and bars were gossiping about me, stood there all thin and sweaty and poor and looking like I was homeless. And all I wanted to do was get back to the youth hostel and hide away in my room from them all.

So I started walking really quickly back down the street and by this point I even think I was mumbling to myself like a nutter just 'cos it was making me feel a bit better and then just as I got to the hostel steps I stopped dead in my tracks 'cos something I saw made me think I'd gone properly loopy over-the-edge crazy insane.

I couldn't believe what I was seeing. It was the most

weirdest most amazing thing ever, ever. Standing at the top of the steps to the youth hostel was Wesley. Wesley Barrington Bains II. My Wesley. Standing there in the doorway to the reception, holding a map and car keys in his hand wearing his New Era cap and some Nike shorts and an England football shirt. Well, my knees sort of went all funny when I saw him. And I tried to say Wesley but I didn't I said, 'Weshhhh' and then my voice disappeared and I could hear Wes saying to the woman on the front desk, 'I know you can't give out names of residents, innit, but this is an emergency! Shiraz Bailey Wood! Have you heard of her, innit?'

Then he spotted me and I started crying and he walked down the steps and he put his arms around me and gave me a big cuddle and I says, 'Wesley what are you doing here?!'

'Well I've come to take you home, Shiz, innit,' he said, still holding me.

And I don't remember much after that. We got all my stuff from the youth hostel and put it into the back of Wesley's hire car and and then we went to the hotel that Wesley had booked into near the airport and Wesley ran me a big bath and I lay in it for ages and he even bloody handwashed some of my clothes and stuck them out on the balcony to dry. Then he took me down to a café and bought me the biggest full English breakfast ever.

Wesley's not mentioned nothing at all about Sooz and what she thinks of all this and I haven't asked him and we've not kissed or nothing like that 'cos I know he just wants to be friends, but I want him to know that I'll never ever forget this day and I bloody love him.

I love you, Wesley, innit.

MONDAY 26TH JULY

Carrie was let out of prison on bail today. She's out. She's bloody free! CARRIE IS FREE! It's like a massive weight has been lifted from my shoulders. Praise the bloody Lord.

She rang this morning screaming her head off like a loony and crying and squeaking and saying that Barney had paid a really good Spanish lawyer to fly into Ibiza and represent her and he reckoned the charges couldn't stick against her as Carrie wasn't even carrying the record box when the police raided the villa. Carrie was in the loo doing her make-up. And there were other girls at the villa too and the police weren't even sure which one was which so they arrested them all and that just confused matters. In fact the police had no rock solid evidence that Carrie ever touched the record box so the lawyer thought the charges might eventually be dropped and she'd get a police caution. But Frankie was looking at four years minimum.

Well I danced round the room like a care in the community person on double dose medication when she told me that. Then Carrie told me how much her dad had paid to sort this whole shambles out and I nearly dropped the phone in shock. It cost him nearly eighty-five grand! OMG! Barney's only had to sell his favourite Jag and remortgage Draperville to get hold of the money. Then I asked Carrie what happened to the other girls who didn't have mums and dads with money to help them out and Carrie said she didn't know. They were still in jail as far as she knew. That's really awful, innit?

Carrie says that Barney isn't really speaking to her at the moment aside from in grunts, 'cos he's too angry, but she knows he's arranged for them to both leave Ibiza tonight. Then Carrie said that Barney did say to tell me he was sorry for his carry on the other morning 'cos he wasn't thinking straight and would I like a ticket home? So I says to Carrie, no that's well kind of Barney, but Wesley has got me a ticket to fly home with him tomorrow. Well Carrie gasped when I said that and said, 'Bloody hell, Shiz, how long was I in jail for? When did Wes arrive?'

So I told her the whole story and Carrie says, 'Oh my days, Shiraz, he's a bloody saint that boy, innit?' So I looks at Wes who was just getting out of the shower wrapped in a towel looking all red 'cos he'd been in the sun and I said, 'Yeah. He is. He's a total angel.'

I put the phone down and told Wes the good news and he gave me the thumbs-up and a big hug. Wes couldn't stop saying how bad this could have been and how Carrie was the luckiest girl alive. Then he took me out to a bar and we had fizzy wine with orange juice in it to celebrate and we sat in the sun and got a bit tipsy and Wes told me the full story of how he ended up coming to get me in Ibiza. Wesley said that the first thing he heard about Carrie's drama was when Bezzie Kelleher called him up on Wednesday morning 'cos he'd heard the news on Essex FM.

Then Wesley says Uma called him up doing her nut asking if Wes had any idea where I was 'cos she was trying her best to make extra tips and buy me a ticket home. But Wes didn't have a clue, so then he called my mother and left some messages and then eventually my mother rang Wes back and he had to listen to her for about two hours going totally NUTS about her bloody stupid kids and asking where the hell she went wrong in this life 'cos she'd tried her bloody best, GOD HELP HER SHE'D TRIED, but somehow she had one daughter hanging about with drug dealers and a son in a gang who gets brought home by the police and another daughter who is running about Goodmayes shouting at people about recycling boxes, starting fights.

My mother told Wes that she thought I was staying in a youth hostel in San Antonio, so that's when Wes thought it wouldn't be so hard to find me and he got on to the travel agent and booked himself a ticket and a hire car and packed some shorts in a rucksack and told his boss he needed a few days off 'cos he had an emergency to attend to and then he set off.

So I says to Wes, 'And what did Sooz say to that?' 'Well

not much, innit,' says Wes. 'She just went in a proper strop with me. Sooz ain't, erm, living in my flat any more. She's gone back to live at her mother's, innit.' I changed the subject then 'cos I didn't want to look like I was happy about Sooz going, but I really am. I am OVER THE BLOODY MOON.

So I asks Wes what he thinks about the whole Murphy being a gangster thing and Wes says he don't really know what to say but he reckons we should keep an eye on it 'cos Murphy's going to get stabbed the way he's carrying on. Then Wesley told me that my mother had been quacking on to him how she was bloody livid at that Ritu girl for breaking Murphy's heart and that she had 'found Ritu's email address and sent her a bloody angry emaily thingy to China, or wherever she was from, telling her all the hassle she'd caused.'

Me and Wesley were laughing our heads off at that. Where the bloody hell did my mother send the mail to I wonder? *Ritu@chinaorwherever.com*? HA HA HA. My mother sending emails is just bare jokes full stop. Like, of course Ritu got that email. Bless my mother, she is trying to live in this century.

Me and Wes sat in the bar for ages today laughing and chatting about all this and all about the old times back in the day when we first met. We even had a little kiss. Nothing big. He's only just split up with Sooz, so I don't want to get him on the rebound. It was still amazing though. This has got to be one of the best days of my life.

TUESDAY 27TH JULY

10pm – Thundersley Road, Goodmayes.

I am home!! It has been ONE HELL OF A DAY for loads of reasons. Me and Wes flew home on the 7am flight out of Ibiza to Heathrow this morning. The flight was well hectic 'cos there were loads of kids who'd come straight from nightclubs and got on the plane and they were all totally off their heads so the air hostesses had to turn off the seat entertainment 'cos people were dancing on their seats and waving glowsticks and blowing whistles. Me and Wesley didn't mind about that though. It was bare jokes. We were both in a really good mood. We got back to the airport and picked up Wesley's banana-yellow Golf and set off back to Goodmayes listening to our favourite Usher CD and singing all the words and laughing at each other's bad singing.

I couldn't believe my eyes when we got back to Thundersley Road 'cos there seemed to be some sort of bloody street party going on. Our house had balloons and a big pink sparkly banner across the front saying 'WELCOME HOME SHIRAZ!!!' and my mother had her wallpapering table in our front garden covered in plates of pork pies and pakoras and prawn ring and all sorts of other Iceland stuff we normally only get at Christmas.

My mother was in her slippers and some curlers by the table trying to chase the Brunton-Fletchers' Staffies who were trying to nick her sausages on sticks. And Cava-Sue was there too holding Fin in one arm shouting at Lewis who was up a stepladder, 'Lewis, that end of the banner isn't straight! It needs to be twenty centimetres down! Come on, Lewis, I want this to look good. Think of the trees that died to make that cardboard!'

So I get out of the car and my cheeks feel all funny like I might cry and my mother sees me and goes, 'Sheeeeee's heeeeeeeeeeeeeeeere! SHIRAZ IS HEEEEEERE!' And then everything goes a bit mad. Murphy appears at the upstairs window and switches on some loud dubstep and my dad rushes out of the front door with all his hair combed to the side like it's a special occasion and our silly fat Penny is running about barking and lying on her back with her feet in the air. Then Clement and Nan appear and Mrs Reema arrives with a big plate of onion bhaji and everyone is hugging me and laughing and soon the whole bloody street seemed to join in the party and no one minded when the Brunton-Fletchers turned up smoking blunts or when old Bert showed up just in his underpants and a raincoat, or when Wesley and me had a snog in front of everyone right there in the street. It was a party after all. All sorts of things happen at parties. I think we were all a bit drunk.

Anyway, just as me and Wes finished snogging a really weird thing happened. A mini-cab pulled up in Thundersley Road right outside the house. And this little dark-haired girl got out and went to the boot and got out a big suitcase. Then she looked around at everyone until she spotted Murphy sitting quietly on a seat by himself looking sort of sulky and she shouted really loudly in a Japanese accent, 'MURPHY! WHAT DO YOU THINK YOU ARE DOING? YOU NOT A GANGSTER! YOU RUIN YOUR LIFE! I NO PUT UP WITH IT! I MAIL YOU AND TELL YOU I LOVE YOU AND YOU NOT BELIEVE ME, WELL NOW YOU DEAL WITH ME IN PERSON IF YOU THINK YOU SUCH A TOUGH MAN! WHAT YOU SAY TO THAT, HUH?' Well Murphy stood up to try and hug her but she just whacked him one, like a proper chop on the arm like bloody Jet-li or something.

I think I was wrong about my mother and her email to Japan. It appears that Ritu did receive it after all. And now Ritu is back in Goodmayes and she says she's staying, in her words, 'for forseeable future'. As far as I remember before I went to Ibiza, Thundersley Road was FULL. There's no bloody room for any more houseguests! Oh well, we always manage don't we. Somehow. OH MY LIFE.

WEDNESDAY 28TH JULY

I went round to Kezia's flat today to see her and Tiq and tell her I'm here for her if she needs me, 'cos I'd just heard her news. Kez is pregnant again. She's not sure how far gone at the moment 'cos she's not had any tests. She's just done the wee on a stick that you buy from the chemist. Kez says she wishes she knew whether she was months or weeks preggo 'cos then she'd have more idea who the babyfather was.

So I said to Kez, ''Ere, do you think you might have been pregnant before you went to Ibiza?!'

Kez says, 'Erm, nah. Well I dunno. I hope not anyway 'cos then the babyfather will be Travis who's the area manager for Bargain Booze and he's white and to be honest I'd quite like another brown baby to match Tiq. Not being racialist or nothing.'

Me and Kez had a think about who else might be the babyfather and we came up with quite a long list of possible suspects. I felt quite sad, but Kez seems quite chilled out about it even if her mother Marlita has gone MENTAL. Marlita says that Kez won't be going on any more holidays for a very, very long time. Marlita says Kez could have caught anything, NOT JUST A BABY, but Kez wasn't really listening to her to be honest.

I left Kez's flat at about 7pm and the lift was broken and there was smashed glass on the stairs and I thought 'Oh my dayz, how is Kez going to get two babies down the steps?! And Clinton ain't even here to thief her a bigger pram.'

Anyway, I'm lying on my airbed now in my old room and Uma's just called for a chatter. Uma sounded proper happy tonight. She's moved into a new flat with another croupier called Joy who she works with. Uma loves her new job and she seems to think Joy is 'really lovely' so I'm happy for her. Joy even drove Uma up to visit Clinton in Chelmsford jail this week which was really good of her. I'm glad she's got a friend. I don't like thinking about Uma all by herself in London 'cos it's not like she ever had a boyfriend.

OMG, this house is bare noisy tonight 'cos Ritu and Murphy are both laughing next door and Fin is screaming and my mum and dad are watching *American Idol* downstairs at full volume and Lewis is outside with his mate fixing a bloody motorbike. My mum said to Ritu this morning that she could only stay here if she got herself a job and didn't become 'another bloody burden'.

So Ritu went straight down and spoke to Mario at Mr Yolk and got herself a job as a waitress. Apparently that Polish Agnieszka girl qualified as a nurse and didn't need the job to pay her way through her studies so Mario had a vacancy.

My mother just scowled at me when Ritu said that. I knew it wouldn't be long before Mum started jarring my head about what I was going to do with my life. I think she's done well to keep her trap shut for two whole days.

AUGUST

SUNDAY 1ST AUGUST

I went over to Draperville tonight to see Carrie. I haven't been over to Carrie's place since all the prison thing happened. I felt proper awkward about it. I suppose deep down I do feel a bit responsible for what happened to Carrie 'cos I was supposed to be looking out for her. I promised Barney I would. I still don't understand why I never listened properly to the little voice in my head telling me that DJ Frankie was dodgy. 'Cos that was my gut instinct all along I suppose. Frankie never seemed like a normal holiday maker. And where did he get all that cash from? I reckon the one thing I've learned from this whole experience is that I should listen to my gut instinct and go with that. It's like that day last year in London when I let my Wesley drive off back home to Essex and start getting serious with Sooz. I knew from the minute I shut my front door that I was being a total knobend, but I didn't do nothing about it. Why does it take your brain so long to catch up with your gut instinct?

So I arrived outside Draperville and first thing I notice is it's still called raperville as the 'D' is lying looking proper sorry for itself on the path. I picked up the D and carried it under my arm down the gravel driveway and

Alexis the Chihuahua comes running out being all yappy and annoying wearing what turns out to be a Miu Miu jacket that Maria Draper has bought online just this week. Not that it stops the stupid dog dragging its bum right down the white hallway carpet the moment I get inside the house.

'Hello, Barney,' I said to Carrie's Dad who was sitting in the lounge on his massive leather chair watching his fifty inch widescreen telly, 'Your letter D has fallen off again. I just found it outside.'

'Oh bloody hell,' he says, 'Never mind, just put it down there.'

I felt really nervous talking to him like he might shout at me again, but he didn't, he pressed pause on his Sky Plus and started to grin.

'So anyway, Miss Shiraz Bailey Wood, it's good to see you again!' he said.

'Thanks,' I said, 'You too.'

Well we both didn't know what to say for a bit then, but eventually he says, 'Look, Shiraz, I've got to apologise to you for losing my rag in Ibiza. I'd lost my marbles. I honestly had.'

'Oh no worries,' I said. 'It was a bit of a mental time. I weren't thinking straight neither.'

Barney looked relieved when I said that. 'She's up there now sulking with me!' Barney says pointing up at Carrie's room. 'She's in the huff.'

'What? Carrie ain't speaking to YOU!' I said. 'Why?!'

Well, Barney started to laugh then. 'I sold her Singstar machine, didn't I?' he says. 'Well actually, I didn't even sell it. I bumped into your big sister Cava-Sue down the shops the other day and she said I should put it on, what's it called? Freecycle? Where you give things away? It's gone to a Children's Home. Ha ha ha! Thank God I don't have to listen to that bloody racket any more!'

'Barney!' I said with my surprised face on. 'I thought you said she was a solid gold talent?!'

'Oh well,' Barney tutted. 'I try to bloody encourage her, don't I? I just want her to find something she wants to do and be happy.'

To be honest I couldn't say anything to that 'cos it's not like I'm a shining example of having my life worked out for me, am I?

'Honestly, Shiraz,' Barney went on. 'The women in this house are driving me MAD! I've just bailed my daughter out of jail which has cost me a bloody arm and a leg. And look what my wife has just spent almost twenty grand on!' Then he stands up and walks over to the doors of the dining-room and opened them both so I could see the banqueting table. The entire ceiling of the room was covered in weird long white shards of plaster, hanging down, covered in twinkly lights.

'What . . . are . . . they!?' I said.

'They're porcelaine stalactites, Shiraz. All the footballers are getting them in their banqueting rooms according to my Maria, who read it in *Hello* magazine.

And now we've got them too,' says Barney.

'Wow! They're proper . . . erm . . . different,' I said, wondering if Maria might have had a mentalist fit while me and Carrie were away. Had to be, innit.

'I know, Shiraz. That's what I said . . . but it keeps my missus happy and when she's happy, I'm happy, so therefore I won't complain.'

Then he sat back down, cracked open a beer and carried on watching his West Ham game, looking quite content. I felt a lot better that me and him were friends again. He's a good bloke is Barney. So then I went upstairs to find his daughter.

'Aight, Cazza,' I said, walking into Carrie's room. She was lying on the bed looking at her Macbook Air, bleaching her moustache and drinking a Diet Coke through a long straw.

'Aight, Shiz?!' she said. 'I thought I heard you arrive ages back, where've you been?'

'Oh I was talking to your dad,' I said. 'Oh, THAT PIG?' Carrie snorts. 'Well I feel well sorry for you. He's a monster! I don't know how much longer I can stay living here. It's worse than prison!! Honestly, Shiraz, he is driving me round the bend!'

Then Carrie's phone rang and she answered it grumpily and says, 'Yeah? What do you want? Yes I am still angry. Yes I am. Yes I am enjoying it, thanks for asking. Look what do you want? Food? Oh? Yeah . . . suppose. OK . . . me and Shiraz will have a set meal D if you're putting in an order but can we change the pork balls for chicken in black bean with green peppers? And get some extra prawn crackers and tell them we want Fanta orange not cola. And if you're getting pudding can we have the deep fried battered bananas and a small tub of Häagen Dazs Vanilla? OK? Bye.' Carrie put the phone down and looked at me and had totally lost her drift. 'What was I saying?' she said.

'Oh yeah. You were saying your dad is a monster and you can't live in this prison any longer,' I said.

'I know!' Carrie said, 'Did you know the knobhead gave away my Singstar?!'

So then we both lay on the bed and gossiped for ages waiting for our food to show up.

''Ere, Shizzle, you know who I reckon Kezia's new kid's baby father is?' says Carrie.

'No, who?' I says.

'Clinton Brunton Fletcher,' she says looking at me with her big eyes.

'What? How?!' I says. 'He's been on remand since December! I didn't know she was THAT kind of friend with him?'

'Oh come off it, Shiz,' Carrie sighed. 'Kez is that kind of friend with ANYONE in trousers, innit? Not being funny or nothing.'

I couldn't really argue with that.

'And Kez's definitely been up and visited him on remand before he got sentenced. Kez told me,' Carrie went on. 'And she said the prison officers were proper laid back and let them spend time alone together!'

'Nooooo way, shut up!' I says to Carrie.

'Proper straight up. True fact!' Carrie says. 'I dunno, Shiz, but there's a little voice in my head saying that that baby is Clinton's and Uma's the aunty. There's some bare strong genes in that family, bruv! That's why there's about two thousand of them!'

Then Carrie sat back on the bed looking proper pleased with her theory. I didn't say anything for a while after that. I was sitting there thinking about Kezia marrying Clinton and being Kezia Brunton-Fletcher. Then Clinton adopting Tiq and them doing a double-barrelled name so Tiq is 'Latanoyatiqua Brunton-Fletcher-Marshal-Drisdale'. But my head started to hurt by that point so I stopped thinking about it. God alive! That can't be true though, can it? It can't be Clinton's baby?

So the Chinese food arrived and me and Carrie were stuffing our faces and Carrie was going on about how her whole prison experience has really made her think about life.

'I mean, Shiz, why do all these crazy things always happen to me? Eh?! Why?'

''Cos you're a mentalist with about as much common sense as a damp Always Ultra,' I felt like saying. But I didn't 'cos we were having a nice time.

'I mean honestly, Shiz,' she says. 'The more I go through life and these CRAZY things happen to me, the more I feel totally sure that I was born to be famous!'

''Erm, well, I dunno about that, Carrie,' I said, but she wasn't listening.

''Cos the thing is, Shiz,' she says. 'I am totally unique and a real individual. I mean fair play, I'm not a great singer, but I have OTHER TALENTS. I don't know why I'm not on one of those reality TV shows or an actress or a presenter or something. I should be doing something like that, shouldn't I?'

Well I just sort of laughed a bit nervously at that 'cos this is typical Carrie going off on one. I mean here's me promising our Cava-Sue I'll do two days' babysitting a week to earn some cash and get by and here's Carrie plotting to be a superstar, AGAIN.

'I've just been on the internet looking at this site called ucanbefamous.com and it's full of all these adverts for auditions,' Carrie said, stuffing three prawn crackers into her gob. 'There's all sorts of TV shows that need people! I'm going to start looking properly tomorrow!'

'Oh shut up and eat your crackers,' I said, rolling my eyes to heaven.

MONDAY 2ND AUGUST

Wesley Barrington Bains II came round tonight to collect me in his banana-yellow Golf. The whole Wood family plus assorted guests were whispering and giggling as he arrived, so I went downstairs and put my head round the living-room door and said, 'Yes, you're right everyone. We are back together. It's official. Mother, you can ring the *Ilford Bugle* and Essex FM and get a big shout out if you want. Shiraz and Wesley are bloody back in love!'

Well my mother nearly choked on her Pringles when I said that. 'OH MY GIDDY AUNT!' she said. 'Shiraz! Now that is good news! That's the best news I've heard this year!'

So I opened the door and Wes was standing there in his New Era cap and his blue Hackett shirt and his Evisu jeans and his white Nike trainers, smelling of Kouros aftershave. And he looked at me in my pink hoodie and hoops and pale blue jeans and loads of lipgloss and he says to me, 'Aight, Princess.' And I says to him, 'Aight, Wes.' And he says, 'Coming out with me then, innit?' and I says 'Yeah.' Then I grabbed my purse and shut the door behind me. And we got in the car and he put his hand underneath my chin and pulled it towards him and kissed me on the mouth and says, 'I love you, Shiz, you, daft cow.' And I says, 'Yeah, I love you back, you knob. Let's go and get a pizza.'

So we went to the pizza shop and got a Hawaiian Extra Hot with the jalapeños on one side and the pineapple on the other and then Wes paid for a film on Sky Box Office called *Crash Bang Bloodbath!* which was about a man who steals cars but he's also a Russian spy or something like that, I dunno, I lost track of it about half an hour ago 'cos everyone looks the same.

I don't think I'll watch the end of it. I think I'll just curl up here on the sofa beside Wes and have a sleep. Carrie just left me this well funny message on my phone but I'm far too tired to deal with it now. She was asking if it's true I'm back with Wesley Barrington Bains II 'cos that's what Kezia had just told her. Carrie was saying that she wondered if that meant I was settled now in Goodmayes for ever FULL STOP, as she's been trying to work out what to do with her life and she's got a few proper amazing ideas. Carrie went on about TV, and acting and stuff – just like when I went round to see her and we ate the Chinese. But I was only half listening to the message 'cos I was eating my pizza and anyway, YES, I am back with my Wesley and I love him and I wouldn't do anything to mess that up, not for the world.

But I pressed 9 on my voicemail and saved the message so I can listen to it again properly later.

I mean, I know she's daft, but maybe there's no harm in that is there? Celebrities? Television?

I'll give Carrie a quick call tomorrow.

SHIRAZ
The Fame Diaries

COMING SOON IN
AUTUMN 2008

Can't get enough of Shiraz? Then look out for the first of her slammin' diaries

...TUESDAY – 8PM

Soapstars on Skates is on TV and our Staffy's snout is jammed up my armpit. Dad's got out the Karaoke machine, Mum's setting fire to the kitchen – least that's what it smells like – and Nan has dropped off on the couch. Yeah, BORED!

But hey, Nan's got me a buff leather diary for Christmas! So now, I – Shiraz Bailey Wood – can write down all my 'goings on': hanging round Burger King Car Park in Bezzie's Vauxhall Nova. Falling out with my hippy sister. Trying not to murder my little bruv. Definitely NOT thinking about school...

Keeping it real...

http://shirazbaileywood.bebo.com

Read on for a slammin' extract from
TRAINERS V. TIARAS

TUESDAY 25TH DECEMBER – CHRISTMAS DAY

So much for ramming the word iPod into every sentence since last June.

Nan got me a diary for Christmas! A pink leather one with a proper lock and everything. Nan reckons I should 'write down all my secret hopes and wishes' then hide it in a place where no one will ever find it. She never said why.

I would have asked why but she chucked me it, sank almost half a pint of coffee liqueur, then passed out snoring. She was making a noise like when Mum accidently hoovers our dog.

Well, it's Christmas Day and I've nothing else to do, so here goes . . .

THE SECRET HOPES AND DREAMS OF SHIRAZ BAILEY WOOD AGED 15

- I hope my boobs grow bigger soon and get proper pointy nipples.
- I hope my mum, Mrs Diane Wood, notices the boob growth and stops muttering to my dad, Mr Brian Wood, about taking me to get 'my bits checked out by Dr Gupta'.
- I hope I get a boyfriend this year as there is a running joke amongst my sister, Cava-Sue Wood, and my

brother, Murphy Wood, that I am a lezbitarian.

(Oh and Murphy, if you're reading this, BOG OFF you smelly turd. These are my <u>secret hopes</u>. AND I KNOW IT WAS YOU WHO WROTE 'SHIRAZ BAILEY WOOD FANGITA-EATER' ON THE FRONT OF MY GEOGRAPHY COURSEWORK.)

- I hope I can learn this year how to be nicer to lads in general. I wish I could be a good listener like my best friend, Carrie Draper. I wish I could learn how to flutter my eyelashes and remember funny lines from *Dog the Bounty Hunter* that make boys laugh. I wish I could stop giving boys dead arms and wedgies when they do stuff like fart near me.

- I hope by January, Mr Bamblebury, our headmaster, has forgotten about my part in the Mayflower Academy Winter Festival which resulted in a request for police presence.

- I hope the local newspaper, the *Ilford Bugle*, forgets that our school, Mayflower Academy (formerly known as Marlowe Comprehensive) came bottom of EVERY exam results and behaviour table in Essex. I really hope they stop calling us 'Superchav Academy' soon 'cos now everyone in Essex calls us it and it's totally embarrassing.

    WE ARE NOT CHAVS, RIGHT?

    OK, we're not ALL chavs. Me and Carrie AREN'T anyway. Uma Brunton-Fletcher down the road is a bit.

- I hope my big sister, Cava-Sue Wood, gets over her whiny-ass self and stops whingeing in the top bunk bed about getting a lemon dressing gown and a pink velour tracksuit off 'Santa' this morning. Does she think I'm happy with my Niko trainers off Walthamstow market? Nobody wears Niko trainers at Mayflower. NOT EVEN THE ASYLUM SEEKERS. I'll have to fake another mugging.

- I hope my best mate Carrie hasn't got an iPod off 'Santa'. What is the point in spending all December drawing arrows all over the Argos catalogue if NO ONE TAKES NO NOTICE?? It is so annoy— oh, gotta go now . . . Mum has made something totally minging with tinned ham in jelly and we're all being forced to eat some.

WEDNESDAY 26TH DECEMBER – BOXING DAY

Carrie got an iPod. A black one. A 80gb one that plays movies. It's got a message engraved on the silver bit on the back that says: 'For our special girl Carrie at Christmas from Mum and Dad XXX'.

AND she got a silver teardrop necklace from Tiffany. And a Calvin Klein bra. And a New Look voucher for £50. I'm not jealous or nothing. No way. I'm happy for her.

I told my mum. She was on the sofa feeding Penny, our Staffordshire Bull Terrier, chocolate coins and watching a Jeremy Kyle Christmas special called *Ho! Ho! Ho! Get Out of My Home!*. (It didn't feel very Christmassy.)

Mum tutted. Mum said, 'Them Drapers have more money than sense.' Mum said, 'That girl will be ruined!

Ruined! You mark my words! You reap what you sow! She'll turn on 'em, spoiling her like that all the time!'

Mum didn't explain how Carrie 'will turn on 'em', but I reckon she was hinting that Carrie might become a psycho axe-killer or something. Can't see it myself, Carrie is a right softie. Carrie once gave a homeless outside McDonald's in Ilford her Rolo McFlurry as she thought he was lying down 'cos he was lacking sugar. Carrie didn't notice that he had wee all down his trousers and was carrying a three-litre bottle of White Wizard cider.

I reckon Mum just feels guilty as our presents were a bit crap. OK that's a lie. Mine and Cava-Sue's were a bit crap. Murphy loved his presents. Especially his Zombie Armageddon – Bloodbath II PS2 game. He's been in his room shouting 'Die! Die!' and blasting stuff for two days. Actually, there's another hope for my hope list:

• I really hope Murphy doesn't get into the army when he applies in three years' time, 'cos when I ask him why he wants to join up he says 'cos he wants to invade France and 'stuff it right up 'em'. (And we're friends with France, aren't we?)

11pm – Have just asked Cava-Sue what the point of keeping a diary is. She says it's just like having a blog on your Bebo or Facebook but 'cos you're the only person reading it you actually write the truth, not a load of old crap about having 'da phattest life eva' like everyone does in blogs.

Cava-Sue always knows stuff like this. That's why she's at college.

Can't get enough of Shiraz?
Then look out for the second of her slammin' diaries

OH MY DAYS!

I've only gone and passed SEVEN GCSEs! Dad and Cava-Sue are chuffed to bits. Murphy reckons I cheated. Mum is pulling her best dog's bum face. She's not happy, I can tell ...

So, Mayflower Sixth Form here I come! Time to ditch the gold hoops and the spray tan and get myself a long scarf, some A4 folders and a new pencil case. Shiraz Bailey Wood is entering a new phase. Clever, sophisticated and definitely not skiving off ... Staying real ...

http://shirazbaileywood.bebo.com

Read on for a slammin' extract from
SLINGING THE BLING

TUESDAY 19TH AUGUST

I am the master of my own destiny.

Well, that's what Ms Bracket, my English teacher last year, always says.

'Shiraz Bailey Wood,' she says. 'The sky is the limit for a bright spark like you! You could be anything you want. Like an astronaut! Or a lion tamer! Or the Prime Minister! The only thing stopping you is yourself!'

She used to jar my head sometimes she did. She was proper obsessed about us passing our GCSEs. Ms Bracket isn't bothered about all that 'Superchav Academy' stuff. That's what a lot of snobby newspaper reporters used to call my old school Mayflower Academy, you see. And I'll say it again for the billionth time. . .

WE WEREN'T ALL CHAVS, RIGHT!?

(Jury's out on Uma Brunton-Fletcher, though.)

Ms Bracket isn't prejudiced and stigmatising towards young people like most grown-ups are. Saying that, she doesn't take any of our crap either. Like when I told her me and Carrie didn't need no English GCSEs 'cos we were starting a world famous singing duo called Half Rice/Half Chips.

'Fair enough, Shiraz,' Ms Bracket says. 'But in the

event that you *don't* become the next Beyoncé Knowles you'll need to get a job to feed and clothe yourself! SO DO YOUR COURSEWORK!'

In the end even I had to admit that passing my GCSEs was a better plan if I didn't want to end up flogging the *Big Issue* outside Netto. If you've ever seen that YouTube clip of me and Carrie on ITV2's *Million Dollar Talent Show* you'll know why. Oh my days, that was well shameful.

Ten pounds flaming ninety-two pence we spent on those matching red leg warmers and devil horns, then we only get one verse into 'Maneater' by Nelly Furtado and this snotty looking judge in trousers so tight you could see the outline of his trousersnake tells me I'm singing like someone strangling a donkey.

Yeah, BARE JOKES, bruv. Jog on.

Not like I cared though. I just laughed in his face. He was like thirty-three years old or something. A proper antique. It's not my fault if he couldn't appreciate me being an individual.

Oh well, that's tea break over. Better get back to work.

2.15pm – I don't regret nothing in my life. Nothing. I'm always moving forward me. I'm keeping it real. It's just sometimes, when I'm standing here behind this pan, frying an egg, and I'm proper sweaty and some bloke with a hairy bum cleavage is at the counter moaning on going, 'Ugggh you've made my yolk hard. I wanted it runny. I like my eggs runny!' . . . Well, it's times like that when I remember Mayflower Academy. I think about what a laugh Year Eleven was with Carrie and Luther and Chantalle and Uma and Kezia.

Y'know there was a bit last year when I even started planning to go to sixth form. And I ain't exactly a sixth formery type of girl if you know what I mean.

But I never thought I'd wind up here at Mr Yolk on Goodmayes High Street making Set Breakfast C two hundred times a day for geezers with bigger baps than me.

This was NOT in Shiraz Bailey Wood's life plan.

'EAT LIKE A PRINCE FOR £2!!' That's the 'mission statement' at Mr Yolk. It's written in BIG CAPITAL LETTERS across the front of my T-shirt. I know I look total butterz in it, but my boyfriend Wesley Barrington Bains II says I look hot.

'Wifey,' Wesley says. 'You could put on anything and you'd look buff, innit.'

Wesley reckons I've got it proper cushy working at Mr Yolk 'cos:

1) It's just down the road from my mother's house and,

2) I get free dinner every day and they do chicken tikka Pukka pies and,

3) He can pop in and see me on the way to his plumbing NVQ and get his egg roll.

Wesley don't like his egg runny. Wesley likes his egg yolk quite hard and he likes the ketchup just on the egg white NOT the yolk, with a sprinkle of black pepper on the yolk. The first dozen times I made Wesley's egg I got it wrong but now I make Wesley's egg just perfect he reckons. That's my biggest achievement all August.

I'm dreading picking up my GCSE results next week. I tried my best and everything. I knew that *Jane Eyre* book backwards by May! I used to go to sleep at night and dream about Mr Rochester on his horse, clip-clopping through Romford and scooping me up outside Time and Envy nightclub and taking me away from Essex.

I tried my total best in that exam, honest.

It wouldn't be the first time my best wasn't good enough.

Can't get enough of Shiraz?
Then look out for the third of her
slammin' diaries

It's all change for Shiraz Bailey Wood and Carrie Draper!
We're chucking in school, we're getting jobs in
London and we're leaving Essex FOR EVER!

Oh my days. I am PROPER excited! I'm signing up with a
temping agency while I work on my 'lifeplan'. Carrie's
all sorted for her place at 'Butterz Beauty School'.

I can't wait to share a flat with Carrie!
And I'm taking my diary with me to write about
every second of life in the big city ...

Shizza and Carrie; moving up in the world ...
but ALWAYS keeping it real.

http://shirazbaileywood.bebo.com

Read on for a slammin' extract from
TOO COOL FOR SCHOOL

SATURDAY 1ST AUGUST

10pm in my room – Goodmayes, Essex.

THINGS SHIRAZ BAILEY WOOD WON'T MISS ABOUT 34, THUNDERSLEY ROAD WHEN SHE BEGINS HER SLAMMING SUPERFLY NEW LIFE IN LONDON WITH CARRIE DRAPER . . .

* Mrs Diane Wood, my mother, quizzing me 'bout where I'm going, for how long and who with EVERY SINGLE TIME I put on my pink hoodie and hoops.

* Miss Cava-Sue Wood, my pregnant sister, quacking on about her 'tingly nipples' and her weak 'pelvic floor' and making us watch screaming women with their knees by their ears on the Baby Channel when I'm trying to eat my Bombay Badboy pot noodle.

* Penny, our morbidly obese Staffy, waking me up for her breakfast at 6am on Sunday mornings by squeaking her squeaky Bart Simpson doll. Then trying to eat my toe-jam.

* Murphy Wood, my little brother, in the room next door to mine, shaking his bed proper quick for four minutes every night before he falls asleep. What is he doing???

* The sound each day at approximately 8.10 am after my father, Mr Brian Wood has visited the lav, when he shouts 'Woo-hoo! No-body light a match!'

* Wesley Barrington Bains II, my ex-boyfriend texting 'the luv hour' on Essex FM five times a week dedicating the song 'Lonely'by Akon' to 'his little shorty shizzlebizzle who he's gonna miss so much, innit.'

Wesley, bruv, we iz OVER, YOU GET ME?

* I won't miss my Aunty Glo coming 'round our house every Saturday night with a ropey movie she's bought off those Vietnamese geezers in ASDA car-park and her bloody karaoke machine. There will be NO karaoke Westlife in London.

* Most of all I won't miss the fact that nearly all these clowns mentioned above have the flipping BRASS NECK to treat me like I'm still a kid when I, SHIRAZ BAILEY WOOD am seventeen years old! I'm practically a bloody woman. Deal wiv-it!!!

Well, asta la vista Wood family! Ha ha LMAO! I'm moving

to London with Carrie Draper! Laterz Goodmayes! Goodbye Superchav Academy! London babeeeeey. Yeeeeeah!

4 am – My bedroom – still awake.

Oh my days. I totally can't SLEEP. I mean, it's not like I'm bricking it about moving to London or nothing. No way. I'm Shiraz Bailey Wood – I'm nails me. It's just I've been thinking about stuff I might miss if I leave home . . .

STUFF SHIRAZ BAILEY WOOD WILL POSSIBLY MISS ABOUT 34, THUNDERSLEY ROAD WHEN SHE BEGINS HER SLAMMING NEW LIFE IN LONDON WITH CARRIE DRAPER:

1. I'll miss when Nan and her husband Clement come over on a Sunday and Nan roasts a chicken and some spuds and she makes all the outside of the spuds proper crispy and they soak up the gravy well nice and she even roasts a few extra ones and leaves them on a saucer for me in the fridge to microwave on Monday.
(NOTE: Must find out what food is on offer in London. Will I have to live on those toasted ham punani things from Starbucks? Christ on a sledge – I hope not. I had one of them on a Geography trip once. It tasted like old badger muff).

2. I'll miss it when me and Cava-Sue go to Spirit of Siam Chinese together to fetch the family's set meal D and we always buy a SECRET EXTRA SPRING ROLL out of Mum's money to eat on the way back and we laugh like mad 'cos greedygob Murphy ain't getting any of it. It is the BESTEST tasting spring roll ever.

3. I'll miss the times when I paint Mum's toenails for her before she goes somewhere special like Goodmayes Social, 'cos it's not like we get on that well usually, but just for those five minutes we're like bezzies and Mum always fiddles about with my hair and I always call her feet 'hooves' and she laughs her head off. Then afterwards mum dances up the stairs with bits of tissue between her toes singing 'I'm Too Sexy For My Feet' and I wolf whistle her. I'll miss that.

4. I'll miss when me and our Murph watch EastEnders and we pretend that we know the plot already. Like Murph says, ''Ere Shiz, I KNOW what happens tonight! The Vic gets hit by a meteor!'
    'Oh really Murph?' I say, 'Well I know what happens tonight! Scientists find out that Phil Mitchell's head is made of Dairylea cheese!' Then we laugh and laugh. No one else finds it jokes. Only me and Murph.

5. I'll miss the times when it's raining on a night and I'm sitting indoors in my room reading *Heat* and our Penny

mooches in and curls up under the duvet like a hot water bottle and we end up asleep, with her head on the pillow snoring. Silly fat Pen.

6. I'll miss when my dad winks at me when I'm on my way out to Ilford Mall and slips me a fiver and says 'Don't tell yer mother, you'll get me shot!'

7. I've got a feeling that I'll *really* miss Wesley Barrington Bains II.

Yeah. I know. I know I say we've OVER. But it ain't TOTALLY over is it? I mean, we don't snog each other no more or nothing but we're still proper good mates. We have been since back in the day. I love my Wesley to bits.

I just don't love him like, y'know, THAT. Least I don't think I do. Or do I? No . . . I don't. Especially now his hair is getting a bit of a sunroof on the top where his head is poking out. Bless. But I really don't think I still love him. Do I? Oh my life. I'm proper confused.

My mother – who is a world authority on EVERYTHING – reckons first love is the deepest. My mother reckons you always care about them a little bit. My mother knows this 'cos her first love when she was sixteen was this geezer called Trevor from Chadwell Heath who she binned 'cos she fancied my dad more 'cos my dad had a Mini Cooper and liked going down

Southend while all Trevor had was eczema and a pet ferret.

So anyways, my mother reckons you never stop caring 'bout your first love. 'There's always a spark,' my mother says. Whatever that bloody means.

What if I don't meet anyone else who properly gets who I am in London? What if all I meet is snotty folk who think I'm just a chav?

But HANG ON A MINUTE, why do I bloody care if they do? I'm only keeping it real! And where will me and Carrie live? And what sort of job will I get? And And why, oh, why does Aunty Glo reckon she can sing all the hard bits of 'Living La Vida Loca' when she actually sounds like one of them Oods off of Dr Who with its wibbly things in the TARDIS door?

And why is this house so noisy!!? And why does London not seem like a very good idea no more? And why have I got the bogtrots coming on? Is it 'cos we all had our dinners out of the 'Oops! Reduced' section of Asda again? And what is my mother's OBSESSION with making the Wood family eat nearly out of date pork products that no one else in Essex wants – not even folk who pay with council tokens!!?

And why is my life always filled with far more questions than answers?

And when I move to London, will I ever get the proper bling-bling, mega life I've been dreaming about? Or will I end up like a crack-head homeless who sits by cash machines with pheggy bits round their mouths and golden crispy patches in their arm-pit region?????

Right, that's it. I'm texting Carrie first then when I wake up.

I'm bloody staying in Goodmayes.